Emily could not breathe. Her skin turned cold, freezing cold, then burned with a pink flush.

David. It was David, here, not twenty paces away from her.

He had changed from the boy she knew all those years ago. That boy had been tall and greyhound-lean, with overlong black hair and eyes too large for his oval face. Now he was even taller, but with broad shoulders and powerful arms pulling against the expensive fabric of his coat. His hair, still a shining blue-black, was impeccably cut and brushed into place, and his skin was a clear, dark olive, not burned by the Calcutta sun.

But his eyes—his eyes told her that this was indeed David. They were as dark-bright as a starry sky. Her breath caught, and she could not move.

She almost called his name aloud, but caught it the instant before it escaped. She whispered it in her mind instead. *David. David, you're back.* A ridiculous smile caught at her lips, and that she could not suppress. Her head whirled in sudden, giddy excitement.

Praise for Amanda McCabe
and her Regency Romances

"Refreshingly original and wonderfully written."
—Under the Covers

"Unique and charming."—All About Romance

"Thoroughly enjoyable."—*Rendezvous*

"An extremely talented new voice that should find an enthusiastic welcome from readers."
—*Romance Readers Today*

The Star of India

Amanda McCabe

A SIGNET BOOK

SIGNET
Published by New American Library, a division of
Penguin Group (USA) Inc., 375 Hudson Street,
New York, New York 10014, U.S.A.
Penguin Books Ltd, 80 Strand,
London WC2R 0RL, England
Penguin Books Australia Ltd, 250 Camberwell Road,
Camberwell, Victoria 3124, Australia
Penguin Books Canada Ltd, 10 Alcorn Avenue,
Toronto, Ontario, Canada M4V 3B2
Penguin Books (NZ), cnr Airborne and Rosedale Roads,
Albany, Auckland 1310, New Zealand

Penguin Books Ltd, Registered Offices:
80 Strand, London WC2R 0RL, England

First published by Signet, an imprint of New American Library,
a division of Penguin Group (USA) Inc.

First Printing, October 2004
10 9 8 7 6 5 4 3 2 1

To the "Hyde Park set"—Diane Perkins, Julie Halperson, Deb Bess, Gaelen Foley, and Brenda Hiatt. I can't believe it's been a whole year since we trekked through Hyde Park and Mayfair! You were the best pub mates ever—and we even found St. George's!

And to everyone on the Splendors of the Regency tour—it was once in a lifetime.

Author's Note

In the course of researching this book, I came across many fascinating sources that I hope may be of interest to people who would like to read more of India, jewels, or the Elgin marbles (in fact, I had to force myself to stop researching and start writing!). The following were some I found to be useful:

Barr, Pat. *The Memsahibs*. Random House, 1989.

Cook, B.F. *The Elgin Marbles*. British Museum Press, 1997.

Dalrymple, William. *White Mughals*. Viking, 2003. (Highly recommended!)

Durbar, Janet. *Golden Interlude*. Academy Chicago, 1986.

Kincaid, Dennis. *British Social Life in India*. Routledge, 1973.

Rushby, Kevin. *Chasing the Mountain of Light*. Palgrave Macmillan, 2001. (Great book about the gemstone industry, history, and lore of India. The tale David tells Emily about the Star is based on a legend about the Koh-i-noor diamond.)

Tytler, Harriet. *An Englishwoman in India: The Memoirs of Harriet Tytler, 1828–1858*. Oxford University Press, 1986. (Fascinating diary of an officer's wife who lived through the Sepoy Mutiny of 1857.)

I also want to give my deepest thanks to author Meredith Bond, who gave me much advice and help in the course of writing this book, and also to her daughter Anjali, for allowing me to borrow her beautiful name!

From the catalog of the
Mercer Museum, London, 2004

It is said that sapphires are the symbol of love and purity, and the Star of India is a prime example of such a legend. A thirty-carat, flawless oblong Burmese sapphire surrounded by diamonds, it was mined in the seventeenth century and originally placed in a shrine to the god Shiva near Calcutta. In the eighteenth century, it was removed from the temple and gifted by Gayatri, daughter of the Maharajah of Ranpur, to her husband, the English Earl of Darlinghurst. It is not known how the princess obtained the Star from Shiva, but it is said that a curse followed the sapphire and was responsible for Gayatri's early death and the Star's dispersal. The jewel was then owned by the Duke of Wayland, and was sold by his oldest son to Sir Charles and Lady Innis, a wealthy merchant family. Both the duke and his eldest son met early ends, and the duchess spent much of her life wheelchair-bound after a hunting accident. The Mercer Museum obtained the Star from the Innis family during the Regency period. It has resided here ever since, as the centerpiece of the Gemstone Collection and one of the foremost sapphires in the world.

In 1991, a jewel thief was killed by falling through a skylight while attempting to burgle the Star. Has the curse followed the Star here? Well—that remains to be seen.

Prologue

Two Hundred Years Earlier

"*Y*ou can't catch me!" Lady Emily Kenton called gleefully over her shoulder, as she dashed down a hillside into a beckoning green meadow. She might only be eight, but she was fast and she knew it. Racing after two older brothers had made her strong and quick, not to mention impervious to teasing and hair-pulling. Now she ran from her best friend, David Huntington, son of their closest neighbor, the Earl of Darlinghurst.

She heard his answering laugh on the wind. He was thirteen now, older than her and much taller, but she knew he did not *let* her win the race, as her brother Alex often did to humor her. That made the victory all the sweeter.

She neared her favorite tree, a spreading, ancient oak, and reached up to grab a stout, low-hanging branch. She pulled herself up onto it, and then onto the next level. She heard the hem of her muslin skirt tear, and knew that she was in for a scolding from her governess, and probably her mother, too. But that did not matter—her heart was bursting with exhilaration and good fun. Being a girl was sometimes so tedious, with music lessons and stitching. She had to seize her enjoyment where she could, out in the sun and the wind.

She came to a rest on the branch, and leaned against the rough tree trunk to catch her breath. Her pale yellow curls escaped from their confining ribbon and fell into her eyes. She pushed them back, and grinned down at David.

"Do you concede?" she called to him.

He braced one arm against the tree and grinned back at her. The sunlight glinted on his overlong crop of hair, turning it the rich blue-black of a raven's wing. Really, Emily thought, he was the most handsome boy she had ever seen, with his dark eyes and tall figure. Except for her father and brothers, of course.

"I concede, my lady," he said. "You are a veritable Atalanta. Now, will you come down from there?"

Emily slid down to sit on the branch, letting her legs dangle. "Oh, I don't know. It is very comfortable up here. I have a lovely view. Why, I can see your house from here, I vow!"

"Then I will just have to persuade you." He leaped up and caught one of her slippered feet, pretending he would pull her to the ground.

Emily giggled, and kicked out at him. "No, no! I will come down." She leaped to the lower branch and then to the ground, where she collapsed onto the grass. David sat down next to her, stretching his long legs out before him.

"You grow faster all the time," he said, admiration in his voice. "I shall need golden apples to keep up with you."

Emily flushed warmly at his praise, but she shrugged as if it was nothing. "I have to be fast to keep out of the way of Damien and Alex."

"Do your brothers tease you a great deal, then, Em?"

"Damien, yes, when he is around, which isn't often these days. Alex, never. He is teaching me to use a sword, much to my mother's dismay. But it is always useful to be able to outrun them!"

"Swordplay, eh? Then you will be even more fearsome, my little Boudicca!"

Emily laughed in delight at his use of their special nickname—they had been reading Ben Jonson's *The Masque of Queenes* together, and the tale of the fierce Iceni queen was her favorite. How she adored it when he called her Boudicca! It made her feel she *could* be brave and strong, even when her family treated her as a helpless infant who must be sheltered.

Her parents and her brothers (or at least Alex) loved her, she knew that, but to them she was their little baby daughter, to be coddled and protected. Only David spoke to her as if she was an intelligent person, a person who could understand books and art and even swordplay and footraces. He had danced with her at her parents' lavish Christmas ball, went riding with her every week over the countryside. He told her tales of his late mother, the beautiful daughter of an Indian maharajah, and of his early childhood in Calcutta before he came with his father, an earl, to England. He was her truest friend.

"*You* need never fear me, David," she said, leaning against his shoulder. "You are my 'parfit gentil knight.'"

He smiled down at her, but she thought there was something sad and strange in his dark eyes. "Is something amiss?" she asked, sitting up straight.

"No, of course not," he answered. "I *will* always be your knight, Emily, I promise. No matter what. Do you believe me?"

He sounded so very serious, so unlike her merry David. She felt a tiny pang of misgiving in her heart. "Of course I believe you. We are friends—we will *always* be friends."

"Yes. Here, I want to give you something." He reached into a small pouch hung on a leather thong around his neck and pulled out a ring. He placed it on his palm and held it out to her.

It glittered in the spring sunlight, beckoning to her. It was a circlet of nine stones—she recognized emerald, ruby, cat's-eye, topaz, blue sapphire, pearl, coral, moonstone, and diamond.

Emily stared down at it, her lips parted with wonder. She knew it was the height of rudeness to gaze at something with one's jaw agape, but she couldn't seem to help herself. It was so very beautiful—more beautiful even than her mother's diamond tiara, and more grand than anything Emily could hope to own before she was grown up.

"Oh, David," she breathed. "It is so lovely!"

"It is the Navaratna," he said, and pointed to each stone with his dark, slim finger. "The stones are for the nine heavenly bodies which rule our destiny—the sun, the moon, Mercury, Venus, Mars, Saturn, Jupiter. That makes seven. The others are the dragon's head and tail— *rahu* and *ketu*. The empty, black spaces in the heavens."

Emily was mesmerized. "All that in one ring?"

David smiled at her gently, and pressed the ring against her palm. "All that. It belonged to my mother. Before she died, she gave it into my keeping. Now, it is yours."

"Oh, no!" As greatly as Emily wanted to keep the ring—as tightly as her fingers longed to grasp it—she knew she could not. It would not be right. She knew how very much David loved his mother, Gayatri, Countess of Darlinghurst, who had died shortly after David and his family came to England. She knew how he must cherish anything his mother left behind. "You must not give this away, David. I can't take it."

She tried to hand it back, but he refused, shaking his head and reaching out to fold her fingers about the ring.

"You cannot refuse a gift. That would insult the giver. You wouldn't want to insult me, would you, Em?"

Insult David? As if she ever could! "Of course not."

"Then it is yours. It will protect you."

"Protect me?"

"That is what my mother said. The heavens protect and bless us." He took the ring and slid it onto her right index finger. It was too large, and slipped about, so Emily tightened her fist to hold it there. It was far too precious to risk losing. "Not that you will ever need protecting, fierce little Boudicca! You will always be able to take care of yourself."

Emily's gaze shot from the ring to David's dark, lean face. He had been behaving oddly all morning, ever since they met at the stream that divided their families' estates, and just then he sounded so sad . . . "I will *always* need you, David!"

"And I will always be your friend," he answered quietly. "If you ever have need of me, send me the ring and I will be here. From the very ends of the earth, if need be."

"But why should I have to send the ring?" Emily cried in growing panic. She clutched onto his arm, holding close as if it was a lifeline. "You are just over at Combe Lodge!"

"Em, please." He took her hands in his, holding her away. "I vow I will always be there for you, no matter what. That is all I meant. We are friends always, are we not?"

"Yes, of course!"

"Then that is all that matters." He pressed a quick kiss to her brow, and gave her a jaunty smile that was more like the David she knew. "Now, I must go home and help my father with some matters; I am sure your governess will be looking for you."

"Yes," Emily agreed reluctantly. Miss Lynn would indeed be looking for her—it was almost time for their dreaded French lesson. Yet she so hated to leave this bright day, and David's company, for the dusty school-room. "But I will see you later?"

He nodded, yet would not meet her gaze. "Later, Em."

She gave him a fierce hug, and leaped up to dash back across the meadow. At the top of the hill, she turned back and waved. David still sat beneath their tree, watching her go.

"Thank you for the ring, David!" she shouted. "I will always treasure it."

"You will not forget what I told you?" he called in return.

"Never!" She gave him a final wave, and spun around to run toward Fair Oak.

She would *never* forget.

"Ah, David. You have said good-bye to young Lady Emily, then?"

David had hoped to slip past his father for the time being, to go up to his chamber and finish his own packing in peace. He had a great deal to think about—a great deal to remember. But apparently that was not to be, as his father caught him walking by the half-open door of the library.

David pushed the door open all the way and stepped into the dark, book-lined room. His mother's black eyes, in the large portrait over the fireplace, watched him closely. "Yes. I told her good-bye."

"Excellent." His father leaned over a crate and carefully placed a stack of books inside, tucking cushioning scraps of muslin about them. Soon, the crate would be added to the dozen others lining the walls. Never mind that the Indian humidity would wilt the pages of the books within weeks.

Surely they would sink the ship with the weight of

their possessions before they could even reach Calcutta, David thought wryly.

"It has been so good of you to befriend the child, David," his father continued. "It must be rather lonely for her, with only older brothers over at Fair Oak."

"It is good of *her* to be *my* friend, as well, Father," David said, feeling strangely defensive at his father's harmless words. Yet how could David explain to him— to anyone—the odd connection he felt to his Boudicca? She was very young, it was true, yet it seemed she held worlds of wisdom in her dark blue eyes. She rode and danced and laughed with great intensity, like no one else he knew, or had ever known. And the way she looked at him made him feel he could be strong and even merry, could laugh, when all he had felt was weakness and sadness for so long. "As you may have noticed, I have precious few friends here in England."

"Eh?" His father glanced up from his task, blinking in the dim light. "Yes, my son, I *have* noticed. That is part of why we are going back to India. I have no family here, and there you can be with your mother's relatives again. There are cousins aplenty at your grandmother's palace."

David opened his mouth to protest, to beg to stay in England. He wanted to remain close to Emily, despite the cold wretchedness of this country and many of its inhabitants. But then he noticed, not for the first time, how pale his father had become, how thin and shrunken. His golden hair was now silver. Once, he had been hearty and robust, turned brown by the Indian sun, full of jokes and laughter. Until his wife died, and they left their home in Calcutta to come here, to their "ancestral home."

England was killing David's father. And David could not add to his troubles with whining and complaints. If his father needed India, needed the sun and the river to feel close to his wife again, then to India they would go.

Even if David had to leave his best friend behind.

"Of course, Father," he said quietly. "It will be good to see my grandmother and cousins again. I will just go finish my packing." As he turned back toward the door, he remembered that he had one confession to make. "Father, I—I did something today you may not approve of."

"And what might that be, David? You have never given me even an instant of trouble before."

"I gave Mother's Navaratna ring to Lady Emily, for her protection."

David closed his eyes against the expected storm of protest. His father held anything that had belonged to Gayatri as sacred. Yet there was no storm, no sound at all. Only silence, and the soft thud of books lowered into the crate.

He glanced back over his shoulder to find his father's head bowed, his clasp tight on the wooden edges of the crate. "Indeed? Well. That *is* fitting, then."

"Fitting?" David asked, puzzled.

"Yes. That we should both leave our treasures in the hands of the Kenton family. They will keep them safe."

Mindful of her torn and muddied hem—and doubly mindful of the scolding she would receive if anyone saw it before she had a chance to change—Emily took off her shoes and crept up the grand staircase of Fair Oak. Thankfully, there was no one to see her except a footman and a maid, who were more interested in flirting with each other than in their employer's wayward daughter. Now, if she could just reach her chamber undetected, and find a fresh frock before Miss Lynn came looking for her . . .

She tiptoed past the open door of her mother's sitting room. It would be the very *worst* if her mother caught her, and gave her a lecture on how a proper duke's daughter should behave! Emily heard her mother's soft tones blended with her father's deep voice, and she quickened her steps past the door. The only thing worse than a lecture from her mother would be one from *both* of her parents!

". . . very sad news about Darlinghurst," Emily heard her mother say. She froze at the mention of David's father, and backed up against the wall so she could hear the rest of the conversation. Miss Lynn said it was very wrong to eavesdrop, but really, how could a girl hope to learn anything if she did *not* eavesdrop? No one told a child anything. The only way Emily knew of her brother Damien's wild ways in London, or her brother Alex's new commission in the Army, was by overhearing.

And now something was amiss with Lord Darlinghurst. Could this be the reason for the sadness she saw in dear David's eyes this morning?

"Yes, quite, my dear," her father answered. "They have been excellent neighbors, and I will miss Darlinghurst greatly at the hunt."

"As will I," his wife said, with a soft sigh. She was quite unusual for a lady in that she relished horses and the hunt—a reason Emily thought it quite unfair that her mother should scold her for lack of ladylike decorum, when her mother herself was out jumping fences! Emily could not dwell on that now, though. She had to find out what was happening with David's family.

"Even if Combe Lodge is leased out, I am sure the new tenants could not be half so agreeable," the duchess continued. "His tales of India are always so entertaining! They could liven up the dullest card parties."

"I fear he was not so well received by others in the neighborhood as he was by us, though."

"Not well received? He is an earl! Surely he is invited everywhere."

"Invited, yes. But not entirely befriended. Not with a

half-Indian heir, and an Indian wife he so obviously still mourns."

There was a long silence from the sitting room, penetrated only by the rustle of the duchess's embroidery cloth, the shuffle of the duke's feet as he paced across the carpet, which was so often his habit.

Emily's mother finally said, "You are right, of course, dearest. Perhaps he will be happier back in India—he does miss it so. Yet I do not understand at all why he would leave such a valuable jewel with you!"

Emily heard a gentle clinking sound, and peeked through the cracked door to see the flash of sunlight on a huge blue sapphire in her father's hand.

She stifled a gasp. The Star of India! It was Lord Darlinghurst's most prized possession. David said it had been a wedding gift from his mother to his father, and was the most valuable sapphire in all of Bengal. She had seen it only once before, locked in a case in the library of Combe Lodge. What was it doing here?

Her father shrugged at her mother's question, and carefully shut the jewel away in a velvet box. "Darlinghurst said there is some dispute with his late wife's family over the true ownership of the sapphire. He does not want to take it back to Calcutta, where it could fall into their hands. He feels it will be safer here with us. And he says you must feel free to wear it, my dear Dorothy! It would look lovely in your hair."

Emily's mother gave a little laugh. "As if I ever *could* wear it! It is too grand for me, and I would be afraid to lose it. But I am happy to keep it safe for him; he has been a good friend to us. Emily will be so sad to lose young David's company, though! They have become such good friends, and I do think she is rather lonely here in the country. Perhaps school would be the answer for her. . . ."

Emily's hands shook, and her stomach ached as if she

would be sick. She did not stay to hear any more. She took off running back down the corridor in a blind panic, uncaring of who might see her.

David was leaving! Going back to India. That was why he gave her the ring, why he seemed so sad and serious today. He was going halfway around the world, and she would never see him again.

She was not thinking clearly at all. No rational images could pierce her mind. She only knew she had to see David, to make him stay here with her.

Emily burst out of the front door past the startled footman and maid, and dashed down the marble steps onto the drive, never slowing. She ran as fast as she could toward the road to Combe Lodge, not noticing the pain in her side, the aches in her leg muscles. She ignored the calls of the farmers she passed.

I must see David, she thought. *I must!*

She swung around the open front gates of the Lodge—only to see a wagon, overloaded with trunks and crates, lumbering its way down the lane. Closely following, coming around to pass the wagon and lead the small procession, was a grand carriage, the Huntington crest painted on its glossy black door.

So it was true. They *were* leaving. David was leaving without saying a proper good-bye.

"David!" she screamed out, afraid he could not possibly hear her. "David, good-bye!"

His dark head leaned out of the window, as the carriage drew farther and farther away from her. He raised his hand in a gesture of farewell, and shouted, "Remember what I told you about the ring, Boudicca!"

Then he was gone. Emily stood there and watched until even the clouds of dust raised by the vehicles had subsided and the road was quiet. She stood there unmoving as a marble statue, as the sun sank lower in the sky and a cool breeze blew up around her.

Her friend was gone. She twisted the ring around on her finger, telling herself that this was all she had left of him. She felt numb now, as if she stood in a snowstorm, but she knew that soon, very soon, the flood of pain would come.

She heard a horse draw to a halt behind her, but she did not turn to see who it was until she felt a gentle touch on her arm. Her brother Alex knelt beside her, his gaze steady and concerned as he watched her. He did not even seem to notice the road dust that marred his new white uniform breeches.

"Are you all right, Buttercup?" he asked softly. "Mother and Miss Lynn are looking for you. It is almost time for tea."

Emily blinked down at him. She felt like she was just beginning to come awake after a very long nightmare. "They have gone away, Alex," she whispered.

"The Huntingtons? Yes, I know. Mother said they were going back to India. I'm sorry, Buttercup—I know David was your friend."

"India is such a very long way away."

"Indeed it is. But I am sure you can write to him once he is settled there. It is not on the moon, you know."

Emily had not thought of that, and it gave her a tiny spot of comfort in her pain. "Do you think I could?"

"Of course. But you must be well when you write to him. He would not want to hear you have caught a chill standing here in the wind. Will you come home with me now, Buttercup, and have some nice, warm tea?"

She nodded slowly, still feeling strangely numb. She let Alex lift her up onto his horse and turn toward home.

I will not forget, David, she thought. *Never.*

Chapter One

"*I*t is true, then, David *shona*. You are leaving us." The soft, dulcet, yet unmistakably imperious voice of David's grandmother Meena floated to him on the warm breeze from her open windows.

David closed the door behind him and leaned back against it, his arms crossed over his chest. He could not help but grin, despite the seriousness of his errand in the zenana. His grandmother could have made a fortune treading the boards, if she had not married a wealthy rajah at the age of thirteen and lived all her life in splendid, if isolated, luxury. Her voice, full of doom, and her pose of weak prostration against silken bolsters were pure drama.

"I am hardly *abandoning* you, *Didu*," he answered. "You have all my cousins still, and a veritable army of servants at your beck and call at all times. I daresay you will not miss me at all."

"Not miss you! *Ish*." Meena flung out one dark, slender, bejeweled arm, her ruby and emerald bangles clinking like the lightest of music. "You are my eldest grandson, my darling, departed Gayatri's child. You are the father of my prettiest great-granddaughter. I rely on you so, David. And now you propose to leave me. To abandon your home!"

Some of David's amusement faded at this familiar litany. She knew very well why he had to go.

He pushed away from the door and moved into the room. His grandmother's personal sitting room was, as always, the very portrait of luxury and comfort. The tiled floor was covered with a carpet woven in rich, jewel-like tones of red, blue, and gold. Scattered about were low tables inlaid with intricate mosaics of flowers in mother-of-pearl, as well as silk cushions and bolsters in green, red, purple, and sun yellow. Heavy wooden shutters were drawn partially over the windows, letting in a cooling breeze but shutting out the worst of the warm afternoon sun. Servants hovered in the shadows, waiting on their mistress's every whim. One of them worked the punkah that stirred overhead.

David came to a halt next to the cushions where his grandmother reclined. The rich silk of her green and gold sari shimmered around her, and her silver-streaked black hair and unlined skin, the shine of her black, kohl-lined eyes, belied her age. She could easily have passed for David's mother rather than his grandmother, and that included her vibrant good health and energy as well as her beauty. Yet she so enjoyed playing the helpless elderly female, dependent on her grandchildren for everything.

What a hum that was. She ran everyone's life in their family, and she well knew it.

"Didu," David said gently. "This is not my only home, as you well know. My father has been dead for years now, and I have neglected my estate and duties in England for far too long. It is past time I attended to them. I have told you all of this before."

"You have a manager for that wretched English estate! A most competent one, by your own account. Surely that fulfills any duty you have there."

"It would be remiss of me not to take a personal interest, as the earl. Indeed, I *have* been remiss. I would not be the honorable man you and Father raised me to be if I did not go back there."

Meena sighed in resignation, as she always did at the conclusion of these disagreements. She sat up against the bolsters, and arrayed the folds of her sari more attractively about her. "You are too tall, David. Sit down before I get a crick in my neck looking up at you, and have some refreshment." She snapped her beringed fingers, and one of the hovering servants brought forth a tray. As the servant melted back into the shadows, Meena arranged the tea things, the bowls of papaya and guava, the plate of sweet *shandesh*.

"Very well," she said, pouring out fragrant mint tea into paper-thin porcelain cups. "I understand that duty calls you back to the land of your father, and I can even agree that you are doing the correct thing, though I cannot like it. I knew from the moment of your birth that you could not be ours forever. Yet why must you take Anjali as well?"

David sipped at his tea, more to give himself time than for the refreshment. This, too, was an old quarrel, one that had been ongoing ever since he announced his intention to return to England. And it was not a quarrel that was as easy or as clear-cut as his own duty.

"Anjali is my daughter," he answered. "She deserves to know all of her heritage, to decide for herself how she will live in her adult life."

Meena snorted in derision. "Decide for herself! A female cannot decide such things."

"Anjali will be able to, when she is older and clearly aware of her options."

"She is nine years old. We should be thinking of a suitable marriage for her, teaching her more of the female arts such as music and embroidery. You should not be dragging her away to the other side of the world, where she will know little of the customs and manners. The English here in Calcutta are so very barbaric. To think that my own granddaughter will learn their ways!"

David set his teacup down with a sharp click. "I will not argue with you about the manners of the English here. But to learn English ways is precisely why she must come to England with me now. She is just a child—she has time to learn anything she needs to know. Her English is excellent; I will hire an English governess for her as soon as we are settled. She is smart and quick—just as her great-grandmother is. She will be fine wherever she goes. And in a few years, if she wishes it, she can come back here."

Meena slumped back against the bolster, a hint of a pout touching her carmine-red lips. "By then, she will be too old for any suitable Bengali match."

David grinned at her unrepentantly. "Then she will just have to marry an Englishman, won't she?"

"And you, David? Will you marry an English-woman?"

His gaze narrowed as he looked into his grand-mother's oh-so-innocent expression. This *was* a new tack of hers. They had not spoken of marriage for him since his wife, Rupasri's, death two years ago. He should have been expecting it. Marriage and matchmaking were Meena's chief delights in life.

He sat back against his own cushions and shrugged carelessly. "I will probably never marry again."

"Not marry again?" Meena's tone was deeply shocked, as if such a thing was utterly unthinkable. "But, David, you are young! You will want a son, to inherit your wealth and title and say prayers for you when you are dead."

"My father has cousins who can have the title, and

Anjali can have my money when I am gone. And I daresay she can say a prayer for my soul as well as anyone."

"Of course she cannot! She is a female."

"You forget, *Didu,*" David said, in a deceptively quiet voice, "that Anjali and I are Christian, not Hindu. Even Rupasri was Christian. God will hear Anjali's prayers as well as He would those of any son."

Meena lapsed into a heavy silence. The point of faith was a sore one with them and always would be. Usually, they just ignored their differences and went on.

Meena was not about to let the issue of marriage go quite so easily, though. "You are a fine match, David. You are handsome, just as your grandfather was, and wealthy. You have a title, which they say the English ladies like."

"Is that what drew my mother to my father? His grand English title?"

"Don't be so impertinent, David! My daughter was a silly, romantic, headstrong girl. Gayatri fell in love with his golden curls and green eyes, and would have no other man. We had begun to arrange a most suitable match for her, but her father foolishly indulged her and let her marry where she would. And now you will be just as indulgent with Anjali."

"It hardly signifies at the moment, *Didu.* Anjali is just a child. Her marriageable years are far in the future."

"But yours are not. You are twenty-eight, David; you have been a widower these two years and more. Anjali needs a mother, and you need a companion. Since you are so determined on your course to leave us and go to England, I suppose it must be an English wife. But even that is better than nothing."

David remembered the chilly reception he and his father had received in England, the whispers about his dark complexion, his "heathen" mother. He shook his head. "I doubt there is any Englishwoman who would have me."

"What? Not one on that entire rainy island? I cannot believe that."

Unbidden, an image flashed in David's mind, a picture of a girl he had known so long ago. Emily Kenton laughed in his memory, the sunlight shimmering on her pale curls, her dark blue eyes full of admiration as she watched him.

I won't forget, she had whispered.

Yes, there *had* been one English girl who stood as his friend. Even after all these years, after everything that had happened—his life in India, marriage to Rupasri, the birth of his daughter—he cherished that memory. With Lady Emily, he had been able to be entirely himself, to forget the bittersweet nature of his life in England, to just laugh and talk like an ordinary boy. She made that time not just bearable, but even—fun. And special.

But that was many years ago. Emily was surely married by now, a grown-up beauty with a family of her own. Perhaps they would even meet when he was back in England, at a ball or a rout or riding across their lands at Combe Lodge and Fair Oak. Yet she would not remember him. Not as he remembered her.

His grandmother watched him with an odd expression on her face, and he realized that his silence had stretched on much too long.

"We shall just have to see once I am settled in England, won't we, *Didu*?" he said lightly.

"Indeed," Meena answered, her tight tone saying she was not entirely convinced by his carelessness. "But there is something else I must speak to you about before you leave, David. Something very important."

She peered up at him with her onyx eyes, and something in their depths killed the flippant remark he had been about to make concerning the relative importance of matrimony. "What is it?"

Meena folded her jeweled hands carefully in her lap. "When your mother married your father, she gave him something—something that was *not* hers to give."

David knew immediately of what she spoke. He had expected her to bring it up as soon as he and his father returned to Calcutta fourteen years ago, yet she never had. She treated his father with the same icy, remote politeness she always had, and she had not even mentioned it when the earl died. Now David knew she had just been biding her time. "The Star of India."

"Yes. The Star." Meena looked more solemn than he had ever seen her, yet her eyes took on a deep glow as she spoke of the Star. "Our family gave the jewel as a sacrifice to the temple of Shiva—it belongs to the god. Gayatri was always a silly girl, and she was overcome by her infatuation with your father. She foolishly took it from the very feet of Shiva and gave it to her husband, in a bid to secure his love to her forever. It was a very great wrong. It brought a curse onto our family—a curse that killed your mother!"

David felt an enormous disquiet at his grandmother's demeanor. She was often full of drama and tears to get what she wanted. Yet now, as she told a very dramatic tale indeed, she was only aglow with quiet intensity, religious fervor.

"Childbirth killed my mother," he told her softly. "She was trying to bring my baby brother into the world."

Meena shook her head decisively. "If she had not stolen the sapphire, your brother would have been safely born and Gayatri might still be with us. It is so written. And then your father left the Star in England, who knows where or with what blasphemous sorts of people! If he had brought it back, we could have returned it to Shiva. Now, the curse—and the duty to erase it—have fallen onto you, my grandson."

So that was it. He was to be the means of erasing a

"curse." David did not believe in such things as curses himself. But he *did* believe in the power of suggestion, and he knew his grandmother sincerely thought she was under a god's curse. A god's displeasure. "What would you have me do?"

Meena took a deep breath. "You must find the Star and return it to the temple. Only then will you and Anjali be safe."

David studied her face carefully, searching for any flicker of deception. "Is this a ploy of yours to entice me to return soon to India?"

She gave an indignant huff, her gold nose ring shimmering. "I might be a foolish old woman, David, but I know when I must be serious! If you are unable to return to India, you must find a safe way to send the Star to me and I will take it to the temple. The most important thing is that you find it. Can you do that for me, David? Please—I beg of you."

He nodded slowly. Begging was not his grandmother's way. This must truly be of deepest importance to her. He did love his grandmother—she had been like a mother to him when his own had died, and he found himself all alone in this strange land. He did not want her mind to be unquiet in any way. "Yes. I will find it for you, *Didu.*"

Meena closed her eyes with a small sigh. Suddenly, she looked all of her years and more. "Thank you, my dearest grandson. *Lokhi mei.*"

David went to her and pressed a kiss to her brow. He did not tell her that he had known all along where the Star was to be found—with Emily Kenton's family.

"Papa, Papa! Here you are at last!" Anjali dashed across the nursery floor to throw her arms around David's waist. "You were gone a very long time."

"I went to see your great-grandmother. She had a great many instructions for our journey." David lifted

Anjali up against his shoulder, even though, at nine years old, she was almost too big for him to do so. She was a tall girl, as her mother had been—tall for a Bengali female, with slender arms and long legs, and a warm, honey-colored complexion. Her hair was the same shining raven black as David's was, as Rupasri's had been, falling to her waist in a shimmering curtain. Yet her eyes were green, as green as emeralds or the English countryside in spring. Those she had gotten from David's own father.

Anjali stepped back from him, a tiny frown puckering her brow at the mention of their voyage. "Yes. My ayah and I have been packing my trunks today, but I don't know what I should bring. What will I need in England, Papa?"

"You may bring anything you like, *shona-moni*," he answered. "Your books and dolls and clothes—everything."

"Ayah says that England is always cold and damp," Anjali said, her tone full of doubt. "I don't think any of my clothes are right. Will you look at what we have packed and tell me? I don't want anyone to laugh at me for not being right."

"No one will laugh at you, sweetest. And of course I will look at your luggage." David took her small hand in his and let her lead him to the trunks arrayed next to the whitewashed wall. They knelt down together on the pink and pale blue carpet, and he watched as she took out and displayed garments and toys for his inspection.

He saw that Anjali was right—few of her clothes would be suitable for an English spring, which was when they would arrive in London. He had always seen to it that she wore English frocks, high-waisted gowns trimmed with ribbons and embroidery, except on very special occasions when she visited her great-grandmother and wore silk saris. But her dresses were all made of light muslins, with tiny puffed sleeves. There were no sturdy wools and tweeds, no cloaks, and only one cashmere shawl. Her shoes were all thin kid and silk. What would protect his girl from the brisk sea breezes they would encounter on the voyage, let alone the winds and rains of England?

He was woefully unprepared to be the sole parent of a little daughter. He realized this as he turned a small slipper over in his hand. Before, his inadequacies had been covered by the advice of his great-grandmother, his female cousins, and Anjali's ayahs. He was a man—he had no idea what wardrobe requirements Anjali might have, what qualities he should look for in hiring an English governess, even what she ate for dinner.

Once they boarded the ship and turned toward Europe, his daughter would be completely dependent on *him*.

"Ayah says I will catch my death of cold in England," Anjali said fearfully.

David felt a deep surge of anger toward Anjali's ayah. This change was hard enough for the girl; how could the woman make it worse by filling her with fears? Anjali was a very sensitive child, and took such things very much to heart. He placed the slipper back in the trunk and turned to give his daughter a reassuring smile. "Ayah is wrong. England is not as cold as all that, though it *is* cooler than Calcutta, to be sure. We will buy you a whole new wardrobe in London, one that is the very height of fashion. You will like that, won't you, my Anjali?"

She gave him a flicker of a smile, and cradled her favorite porcelain doll closer against her shoulder. "May I have a *pink* gown, Papa?"

"You may have as many pink gowns as you like. And a red velvet cloak trimmed with fur, and a bonnet with feathers. Once we are settled at Combe Lodge, we will see about finding you a pony, too, and teaching you to ride. All fine English ladies ride."

"So, I will be a fine English lady? Like Lady Mac-Gregor at Government House?"

David laughed at her doubtful moue, and leaned over to kiss her cheek. "Lady MacGregor is not the *only* English lady in the world, you know! You will be far finer than her. Though you are a very *small* English lady, to be sure."

Anjali laughed, and he reveled in the sweet, sweet sound. Her laughter was too rare since her mother died. "I think I *would* like a pony, Papa."

"I know that this change is not easy, Anjali," he told her. "But England is not such a very frightening place. It has many beauties, and there will be much for you to learn and enjoy there. And you will never be alone. I will always be with you, and you must be sure to tell me if there are things you dislike or do not understand."

"Of course, Papa." She opened her mouth as if to say something else, but then she closed it again, her gaze sliding away from his.

"What is it, Anjali?" he asked her.

"I just—Ayah says that you are going back to England to find me a new mama, because none of the Indian ladies suit you. Is that true?"

Now, where would the woman have heard such a things? David thought wryly. He remembered his grandmother pressing him about marrying again, remembered the lists of eligible ladies his cousins devised. Why would they all think he *must* have a wife? It was maddening!

Then he recalled his utter confusion in the matter of Anjali's clothes. Once they were settled at Combe Lodge, there would surely be other things he knew nothing of, such as housekeeping and meals and hiring proper servants. As Anjali grew older, there would be Seasons to plan, gowns needed, suitable suitors found.

Perhaps a wife would have advantages, then. A comfortable home and a properly raised daughter were no small matters. But—and perhaps this was foolish of him—he did hope for more. He cared very much for Rupasri; she had been a fine lady, and excellent mother to Anjali, accomplished in all the arts of a Bengali lady. Yet their match had been an arranged one, undertaken for the benefit of their families when they were very young. If he married again, he wanted it to be from his own desire only.

But that was a romantic hope, a distant possibility. He had other, more pressing duties to think of. And his life would be theirs for a very long time to come.

David drew Anjali close to his side, doll and all, and said, "We are going to England to see about your grandfather's properties, and so that you can learn more about that side of your family. We have duties and obligations there. That is all." And also to retrieve the Star from the Kenton family. But Anjali did not need to know that. She had never even heard of the Star of India.

"So, I will not have a new mama waiting there?"

"No, *shona-moni*. No new mama waiting at the dock. One day I might marry again. But not soon, and only to a lady who would be a very fine mama indeed. Very well?"

Anjali nodded. "Very well, Papa. Now, will you look at these books? May I take them all with me?"

David watched as she pulled a pile of leather-bound books from one of the trunks, yet he did not truly see them. For the second time that day, he was lost in the mists of the past.

Anjali was nine years old now, very nearly the same age Emily Kenton had been when they parted so long ago. But the two girls were so very different. Anjali was quiet and studious, shy and uncertain, where Emily had been full of vibrant energy and life, always dashing about, always laughing.

Emily would be twenty-two now. Once again, he wondered if she was married, if she had grown into the beautiful, glorious woman she promised to be. A lady like that would be an exemplary example for Anjali, an exemplary, passionate wife for any man.

Would they ever come to meet again?

Anjali settled back for her nap after her father left her, watching the shadows of the punkah move against her ceiling. She bit her lip as she recalled her papa's answers when she asked him about a new mama. He was truthful, she was sure—her papa was always truthful. But she was unsure, nonetheless.

She remembered all the dark-eyed beauties of the town, all the pale English ladies with their bonnets and parasols. Their eyes, whether dark and kohl-rimmed or lightest blue, were wide with sympathy as they looked at Anjali, their lips, some carmine and some shell pink, pursed in coos and murmurs. They patted her head and gave her sweetmeats, whispering all the while, "The poor *lokhi mei*. Her mother has been gone so very long, and she has no lady to teach her proper behavior!"

Several of those ladies, so soft and fluttering in their silks and muslins, had their eyes on her papa. They watched him from under their parasols or behind their ivory screens. They were always trying to gain favor with Anjali's great-grandmother, or even with Anjali herself. But none of them had ever been right for her papa.

Truth to tell, Anjali had never much missed having a mama. Her own mother had died when Anjali was only little, and she remembered her more as a lovely dream than a real person, a vision of gleaming black hair, a whiff of jasmine perfume, a soft voice calling her a *gul-poola mei*. For as long as she could truly remember, her papa had been her only parent, and that was fine. Better than fine—it was perfect.

And she never wanted it to change.

Chapter Two

London, Ten Months Later

*H*er mother always admonished Emily not to eavesdrop, always said she would not hear anything to her own advantage.

The dowager duchess was a very sensible woman, Emily knew that and often took her sage advice. But not in this. After all, how else was she to learn anything, advantageous or not? No one told her anything directly. Eavesdropping had often served her well since childhood.

It served her now, as she leaned against the closed breakfast room door, unabashedly listening to the conversation of her brother Alexander and her sister-in-law, Georgina.

Emily *had* been about to open the door and join them in their meal. Then she heard her name, and paused with one hand on the painted porcelain knob.

"I am worried about Emily, my darling," Georgina said.

"Worried about Em?" There was a sharp click of silver on china, as if Alex had abruptly set down his fork. "Why? Is she ill?"

"No, no, nothing like that. At least not that I am aware of."

"Good. I did not think a lady could be ill and still attend two balls, a musicale, and a Venetian breakfast in a twenty-four-hour period."

"Perhaps that is what I am worried about," Georgina murmured.

"Whatever do you mean, Georgie? Do you suspect she is unhappy about something?"

There was a soft rustle of silk; Emily imagined Georgina shrugging her shoulders. "She does not *appear* to be so. She delves into the social whirl of Town with every appearance of enjoyment. But there is something—something not quite right."

"Georgie, my love, we have been married for years now, yet I confess I still do not always rightly understand you. Emily dances and smiles, and appears for all the world to be a happy young lady. Yet you are worried," Alex said, his voice full of fond exasperation.

Georgina gave a little laugh. "Oh, darling, sometimes I do not rightly understand *myself!* But I do worry about Emily. This is nearly the end of her third Season, and she has not yet found someone she can esteem enough to marry."

"Yes. I sometimes worry about that myself, yet truly, I do not think we have cause for concern at present. You and I were not exactly callow youths when we wed. She has time. And I would not want to see her married to someone she cannot truly love, just because he is suitable or it seems like the proper time."

Amen to that, Emily thought fervently. She remembered the parade of suitors over the past three years. Their number had not been insubstantial—her family title was an old one, after all, and she was well-dowered thanks to the fortune Georgina had brought with her to the family. But most of those men were too old or too young, gambling fortune-hunters, merchants seeking a title, widowers wanting a mother for their twelve children.

There had never been one among them with whom she could make a home and family, whom she could truly love. Love as her mother and father had possessed, or as Alex loved Georgina.

Sometimes Emily watched them as they danced together at a ball, or walked in the garden. They had eyes for no one else, and were always holding hands or linking arms, completely uncaring that it was not the done thing for married couples to be *in love*. She watched them as they played with their children, always laughing together. Emily was happy for her brother—truly she was. He deserved his happiness after long years at war, and Georgina had never been anything but the best of sisters to Emily.

Yet sometimes—only sometimes!—her heart would ache with envy at their romance. When would *she* find love like that? Would she ever? Or did it not truly exist, except in books and for a fortunate few? If she did find it, would she be brave enough to embrace it, or would she run?

But she had thought no one noticed these thoughts. She tried so hard to hide those pangs behind the merriment of the Season, filling her time with shopping and soirees. Emily forgot that Georgina was an artist, that her sharp eyes saw even things that were veiled.

"I would not want to see her wed to someone she does not love, either!" Georgina protested. "I love Emily as my own sister, and I want only to see her happy. If the single life suited her, I would be glad for her to live with us at Fair Oak forever. But I cannot be so selfish. Emily has so much love in her heart. And you have seen daily how wonderful she is with the children."

"Yes. I have." Alex's tone grew quiet and serious.

"So, what shall we do, my love? Send out far and wide for every eligible gentleman to come and present their suit for her?"

No! Emily's mind screamed. It was embarrassing enough to be spoken of like a pitiable charity case. She would *never* want her brother to go barreling about in Society *demanding* that someone marry her.

She shuddered at the very thought.

"Of course not," Georgina answered. "Don't be silly, Alex darling. Perhaps she could come to Italy with us this summer? We always meet such interesting and unusual people there. She might encounter someone more to her taste in Venice or Padua."

"You do have a point, Georgie. Emily did not lead the life of a sheltered young miss for many years. She is too intelligent and shrewd for all these London fribbles. Perhaps a change of scene is needed."

Emily gave a silent, humorless laugh. No, she was *not* as all the other misses in white muslin making their bows at Court and Almack's. During the years before her brother Damien's death, while Alex was away fighting in Spain and Damien was gambling away almost every cent of the Kenton fortune, it was Emily who kept Fair Oak going. She scraped together harvests and saw to it that the roof was patched, the fields plowed, the tenants looked after. She took care of her mother, who was confined to a Bath chair after a hunting accident. She had seen things, been responsible for things, that few young ladies of twenty-two ever were.

Those years *had* been difficult. They had hardened her heart and soul in some ways, but she was also proud of them. Proud that she had managed to keep their home together, and upheld the honor of their name when Damien had been doing his damnedest to destroy it. The Kenton name, the title of Duke of Wayland, was one of the proudest in England, and Emily would do it all again to keep it that way.

But it did *not* make the search for a soul mate easy. Men wanted soft, gentle wives, who embroidered and sang and laughed quietly. *Not* wives who could keep farm accounts like a bailiff and scythe hay under the autumn sun. Not wives who rode and walked quickly and spoke their minds.

Emily almost laughed aloud. Those hard days were gone now. Since Alex married Georgina and restored their grand position, Emily had only to enjoy herself. And she *did* enjoy herself. She loved dancing, and shopping without worrying over what she was spending. She loved riding in the park, and playing with her niece and nephew, and buying her mother lovely little gifts. She had a fine life, and she was a great fool to feel even an ounce of self-pity.

But Italy would indeed make a nice change. Perhaps there, under the warm sun, she could breathe again.

Emily pushed open the breakfast room door and breezed in, as if she had not a care in the world. And as if she had definitely *not* been eavesdropping.

"Good morning, Alex, Georgie," she said, kissing them each on the cheek before she sat down in her place and reached for the rack of toast. "I trust you both slept well?"

As she spread marmalade on the triangle of bread, she noticed the two of them exchange a surreptitious glance over the table. She took a large bite to stifle her chuckles.

"Very well, thank you, Emily. And yourself? You danced every dance at the Michaelson rout. you must have been very tired," Georgina said, passing her a platter of eggs.

"Indeed. I slept like the proverbial baby. I also enjoyed the theater last night; didn't you? Mr. Kean was in

fine form. I do not think I have seen a finer Macbeth."
Emily sipped at her tea, and gave Georgina an innocent
smile.

"Quite, my dear," answered Georgina. "Would you
care for kippers?"

"There was an account of the play in this morning's
Times," Alex said, and handed the folded sheaf of newspaper to her. "It says you were wearing a gown of co-
quelicot muslin with white Vandyke trim. And here I
thought you were wearing red with some sort of jagged
ribbons. I am not very à la mode, am I, Em?"

Emily laughed at his teasing, and skimmed over the
account of the play and its spectators. "They liked
Georgina's silk demi-turban, as well. How gratifying.
What do they say about the Hurst ball? I was sorry we
missed it, but I did promise Lady Michaelson first."

"Oh, it was bound to be quite flat," Georgina said,
with a dismissive wave of her teacup. "Mrs. Hurst has
declared she can no longer serve 'intoxicating bever-
ages' since that dreadful Lord Carteret destroyed her
ballroom last year after getting foxed on her husband's
brandy. So there was to be no champagne at all, only tea
and lemonade. As insipid as Almack's, I vow."

"Heaven forfend," Alex said in mock horror.

Emily read over the particulars of the ball. It sounded
quite as insipid as Georgina described. She started to
turn the page, when another headline caught her attention.

SIR CHARLES INNIS TO DONATE THE FABLED STAR OF
INDIA TO THE NEW MERCER MUSEUM.

The shock of those words was like a dash of cold
water to her face. Emily gasped aloud.

"What is it, Emily dear?" Georgina asked solicitously.
"Some unpleasant news?"

"Oh, no," Emily said quickly. "It is just—I swallowed my tea too quickly." She drew the paper up to cover her expression, and read quickly.

It had been many years since the Star passed from their family to Sir Charles Innis and his wife, yet Emily recalled it as if it was only yesterday. There had been a most dreadful scene.

Emily's father was dead for several years by then, yet Lord Darlinghurst had never sent for the jewel. Nor did his family in India, after his passing. It resided in the library safe at Fair Oak, a silent reminder of their old friendship with their departed neighbors. Emily had loved to think of it there, a shimmering blue link to David and a faraway land she would never see. She dreamed of the day she and David would meet again, and she could give the Star safely back into his hands. It took her away from her everyday life of looking after the estate and her mother and drew her into a dreamworld.

Until the afternoon Damien came riding hell-for-leather up to Fair Oak and took the sapphire from the safe.

Damien did not come often to Fair Oak. He detested the country, and much preferred the excitements of Town. All the better to squander every shilling that was not entailed, of course. The country boasted no gaming hells or brothels. Emily had been only sixteen at the time, but she was already fully aware of all these matters. There was no escaping the whispers of the servants and the neighbors, her mother's weeping despair.

So, that morning, Emily was shocked to see him riding down the drive at Fair Oak. She ran out of her chamber and halfway down the grand staircase, just in time to watch him tear into the library. He had once been as handsome as Alex, tall and dark-haired, but by then he was ravaged by his debauchery. He was heavy with excess fat, his eyes red-rimmed and his jaw slack. He was covered with mud from his wild ride.

Emily's mother, confined to her chair, shouted at him from the doorway of the drawing room. "What do you think you are doing, Damien? Get out of your father's library this moment! You have no right to be in there."

"It is *my* library now, Mother," he shouted back. "As is everything in it. I am the duke now, in case you have not noticed. So, I will thank you to be silent."

Emily's mother gasped in outrage at his harshness. Emily, her heart full of her own white-hot anger, dashed into the library to see him take the Star from the safe. For one instant, she saw the rich glow of its blue fire—then it disappeared inside Damien's greatcoat.

"What are you doing?" she cried out. "How dare you? Put that back this very instant!"

He glanced back over his shoulder at her, his eyes full of bitter weariness. "So, you are becoming a harridan, too, Emily. Just like Mother."

Emily ignored the insult, and stalked closer into the room, her hands curled into tight fists at her side. Her nails bit into her palms, yet she scarcely noticed the pain. "That does not belong to you. It is Lord Darlinghurst's."

"He hasn't been back for it in all these years, now has he? That means it is mine, to do with as I like. And I *like* to sell it."

With that, he left the house, the Star in his possession. Emily's screams and shouts as she chased him down the drive had no impact at all. She never saw the sapphire again; the next she and her mother heard, it had been sold to the rich merchant Innis, who was a great collector of exotic items from other lands.

Now he in turn was selling it, all these years later. Or rather, donating it to the Mercer Museum for their gemstone collection. Emily quickly read over the details, then scanned them again. The Star, which had not been seen since Sir Charles Innis purchased it, would be displayed at a grand ball in his London mansion. Then, after being examined by numerous gemological experts to confirm its authenticity, it would make its ceremonious way to the museum.

"This is terrible!" Emily exclaimed aloud, before she could stop it.

"What is terrible, Em?" Alex asked.

Emily lowered the paper to find him and Georgina watching her intently. She had to tell them *something*. Anything but the full truth.

Alex had been in Spain when the drama of the Star played out, and, as far as Emily could recall, he knew nothing of its history. She told him a shortened version of the tale as quickly as she could.

She did *not* tell him of that other scene in the Fair Oak library, the one that took place almost a year after the day Damien snatched the Star away. Indeed, she hardly liked to recall it herself.

Later, when Emily made her excuses to Alex and Georgina and escaped back to her bedchamber, she collapsed onto her chaise. She stared up at the ceiling, which had been whimsically painted by Georgina herself, but she did not see the cavorting gods and cupids against their blue sky. All she could see in her mind, replaying over and over again, was the day she learned the truth about what happened to the Star.

She had not thought about that day, or the sapphire, in a very long time. At first it was too painful to recall how she, in her helplessness, had betrayed her friendship with David. Later, there were so many other things to worry about. The whole ugly story was hidden deep in her heart—a shameful secret. Now it was returned to haunt her.

She rolled onto her side, and reached inside the bodice of her morning gown to pull out her Navaratna ring, suspended on its long gold chain. She always wore it there, hidden from the world but close to her heart, keeping her safe. Holding the circlet tightly in her hand, she closed her eyes, seeing again the day Damien returned to Fair Oak after stealing the jewel. He was in a terrible condition, his skin gray and clammy, his hair long and tangled, his eyes sunk deep in purple circles. He was so drunk he reeked of it from every pore.

He died only a few months later, but she did not know then how truly ill he was. She only knew that she had to hide him from her mother. Dorothy was weak herself, unable to leave her chair. She did not need to see her eldest son in such a pitiful state.

Emily helped him into the library, watched him collapse onto the leather settee. As she pulled off his muddy boots and drew a blanket up over his bloated shoulders, he caught her hand in his.

"Emily," he said raspily, his breath foul on her face. "You have grown into a pretty lady. If you went to London, you could marry a rich man, raise our fortunes again."

Oh, yes, Emily thought sarcastically. She would go to Town in her mended gowns and old bonnets, with her sun-browned face and calloused hands, and snare a rich man so her brother could gamble and whore some more. In the meantime, her mother would be alone and the crops would wither.

But she just gave him a curt nod, and turned to leave him in his disgusting state. He caught her hand again, holding her where she was. His breath rasped in his throat. She tried to pull away, only to freeze when she felt the cold press of coins in her palm.

She stared down at them. It was gold—more money than she had seen in a year. "Where did you get this?" she gasped. "At the gaming tables?"

Damien gave a rough laugh. "Not at all. Lady Fortune has not smiled on me in months."

"Then where did this come from?"

"Does it matter, Emily? Use it to buy yourself some new gowns. God knows you need them."

Her patience, never great when it came to Damien, snapped. "Tell me where you got it!" she shouted.

He fell back on the settee, closing his eyes with a groan. "I did not steal it, if that is what you're implying, sister dearest. And pray do not shout so—my head is splitting. I made it from the sale of that stone you were so damnably fond of."

"The Star?" Emily gasped, appalled. She tossed the coins back on top of him, as if they burned her skin. She did not even question how he had held onto the money for nearly a year since he took the Star away. "I won't take your ill-gotten gains. These *are* stolen."

"Oh, don't be so self-righteous! You're as bad as Mother. Besides, it is not as you think."

"No?"

"No." He opened his eyes, and gave her a sly, bleary grin. "The stone I sold to that vulgar Cit, Innis, was not the real thing. I sold him a paste copy, and gave someone else the real thing. Clever of your old brother, wasn't it? And here you've been looking down your nose at me for years, like you are so much better than me, so much finer. Yet *you* could never have come up with such a scheme, you prim little hypocrite."

"Indeed I could not," was all Emily could say. Then she ran from the library to be sick, appalled that he could do such a horrible thing. He had stolen the Star not once, but twice. Or was it three times? She could not even count.

He left Fair Oak the next day, and Emily never saw him again. A few days later, a new Bath chair arrived for their mother, along with a length of spangled muslin and new cashmere shawls, no doubt paid for with the money she'd thrown back in Damien's face. To her everlasting shame, she kept them. Her mother needed that chair. Emily also never told anyone the truth about the Star. Such a thing would tarnish their honorable name forever, a name Emily had spent her life protecting.

She remembered the newspaper article, which had said that experts were coming to examine the Star before it went to the museum.

There *had* to be something she could do now! Something that would not upset Alex and Georgina, or disrupt their new, wonderful life. Emily had spent years taking care of her family alone. She could do so now. She owed it to them, for all they had done for her.

She could write to Sir Charles Innis and offer to buy the jewel, of course. And she would. Yet she did not have very much hard currency of her own, and Sir Charles was rich as Croesus. He had no need to sell, and indeed had resisted all offers from many people—even, reportedly, the prince regent—for many years. She needed a different plan.

Emily rose from the chaise, and made her way quietly out of her chamber and up the stairs to the very top of the house. There were attics there, behind the servants' quarters and above the nursery. Fortunately, it was silent up there at that time of day; there were no servants about to wonder why Lady Emily had gone to the attics.

She knew that some of Damien's papers and possessions had been packed into trunks and stored there after his death, with no one sorting through them beforehand. With some luck, she could find something there to tell her where the Star—the *real* Star—had gone.

Chapter Three

"*E*mily, dear, why did you not wear your birthday necklace? It would look perfect with that gown."

Emily heard Georgina's voice, but it seemed to come from a very long distance away, not just from across the carriage. She dragged her distracted attention from the night-dark streets outside the window and blinked at her sister-in-law. "I beg your pardon, Georgie?"

Emily was *not* so distracted that she did not see the worried, speaking glance Georgina shot at Alex. So, they were concerned about her, were they? Was it just that old worry of her lack of a betrothal—or something more? She should watch herself, carefully maintain her façade of cheerfulness. She did not want them to know the truth—not when it was her own problem, her own responsibility.

"I asked why you did not wear the necklace Alex and I gave you for your birthday," Georgina repeated. "It would look lovely with your gown."

Emily pulled her cloak closer about her throat, as if to belatedly conceal the fact that she wore her garnet cross rather than the elaborate web of pearls and diamonds they had given her. It was an exquisite piece, and would indeed have been lovely with her white and silver satin gown. But it , along with the matching pair of earrings, resided now with a jeweler in Gracechurch Street, given in exchange for a genuine sapphire copy of the Star of India.

She touched the tip of her tongue to her dry lips. "I— it is being cleaned."

"Cleaned?" Alex exclaimed. "We just gave it to you last month."

Emily stared blankly at her brother. "One of the stones was loose. I took it to be repaired."

Alex frowned at her. "I thought you said it was being cleaned."

"It will be repaired and then cleaned," Emily said with a little laugh, trying to sound completely unconcerned. She was glad it was dark in the carriage, to cover the hot flush of her cheeks. Alex had always been her favorite brother, her friend and champion. She had never lied to him.

It is for his own good, she reminded herself. *His and Georgina's, and their children's.*

Georgina laid her hand gently on her husband's arm. "It is of no matter, darling. Em has obviously taken care of it all, and there is nothing to worry about. The garnets also look very nice, quite dramatic. Oh, I *do* hope we shall arrive soon, and have no difficulty in getting inside the ballroom! Lady Wilton's balls are always such dreadful crushes, I vow she deliberately invites too many to fit into her house. At least we can be assured of an excellent supper . . ."

Georgina went on chatting about the ball to which they were en route, and Emily turned her attention, with great relief, back to the window. She was tired from the sleepless nights she had endured ever since hearing of the Star, and her head ached with a low, dull throbbing. She did not really look forward to this ball, to all the dancing and the chatter. She had even considered making her excuses and staying home with a book and a tisane, before thinking better of it. When she was alone in her chamber, her thoughts took over, swirling like mad until she wanted to scream with confusion.

At a ball, she would never be alone. She would dance and make polite conversation, and not have to think at all.

Their carriage drew up outside Lord and Lady Wilton's grand London house, signaling the beginning of that mindless evening. There was indeed a great crowd waiting to enter the ballroom, but they moved along briskly, and in seemingly no time Emily found herself in the midst of a knot of revelers.

The ballroom—a long, narrow expanse of red silk wallpaper and glistening gilt trim—was so overrun that the arrangements of hothouse roses and orchids and swaths of greenery could hardly be seen, but she could smell their sweet, cloying fragrance. It mixed with the perfumes of the guests, the warmth of thousands of candles.

Emily felt a bit lightheaded, but she could not have swooned even if she wanted to, she was pressed so closely by her crowd of usual admirers.

"Lady Emily!" Sir Arnold Ellis cried, bowing over her hand. He was one of the most handsome of Emily's suitors, golden-haired with bright blue eyes. Unfortunately, his brains were not as well-developed as his grooming. "May I beg for the next quadrille?"

Before Emily could answer, Lord Pickering slid in and took her hand away from Sir Arnold. Pickering considered himself quite the charmer, and always affected pink waistcoats and jeweled quizzing glasses, along with a multitude of watch fobs. He made Emily laugh, though perhaps not in the way that he hoped to. "I believe Lady Emily promised *me* the quadrille when we met last night at the Hardiman musicale."

Emily recalled no such thing, though Lady Hardiman's daughter's performance at the harp *had* been rather loud and she hadn't heard very much over its strains. But as she opened her mouth to say she did not remember, her hand was seized by Mr. Carrington. He kissed her gloved fingers with his usual puppyish enthusiasm. He was a very sweet gentleman, and not a bad dancer, though she sometimes tired of hearing all about the horses and hounds he kept in the country for his beloved hunting. After what had happened to her mother, Emily *loathed* hunting. "Lady Emily, you will never guess!" he said, in one of his usual non sequiturs.

Emily smiled at him gently. "No, Mr. Carrington, I will not be able to, er, guess."

"There is a *real* nabob here. Fresh from India!"

Pickering gave a disdainful sniff. "There are a dozen nabobs here, Carrington. Why, I see Lord Montmorent right over there, still sunburned from the Punjab."

Carrington shot Pickering a loathing glance, then turned back to Emily. Behind his back, Pickering and Sir Arnold snickered. "Not that sort of nabob. He is, oh, a what-you-may-call-it. A rajah."

"A native of some sort?" Sir Arnold asked, his tone disbelieving.

"Yes! But a rich one. A native and an earl. An English earl." Carrington frowned, suddenly confused. "Is that possible? Can a man be a native *and* English? With a title?"

Emily stared at him, suddenly frozen to her spot. Her stomach gave a little leap, and the ballroom around her seemed to slow to a blurred crawl.

An English earl who was also Indian? Could it possibly be David? After all these years? Surely not. Yet how many other earls could there be like that? It had to be. Perhaps she could see him again—the friend who had lived in her thoughts for so long!

But it had been so very long. Surely he would not remember her. And he would be so very changed *she* might not remember *him*.

Her heart pounded inside her breast, and she pressed her gloved hand against it. There, beneath the satin of her gown, she felt the outline of her Navaratna ring. It was always there, hidden on its chain around her neck, reminding her of the protection of the universe around her.

Carrington peered at her closely, his high brow wrinkling in concern. "I say, Lady Emily, are you quite well? You look very pale."

"Perhaps she needs some champagne," interjected Sir Arnold. "*I* will fetch it for her."

"No! *I* will," Pickering argued. The two of them dashed off in a ridiculous race for the refreshment table.

It would have made Emily laugh, if she had paid them any mind at all. She stared at Carrington, and swallowed hard past the dry lump in her throat. "I—I am quite well, thank you, Mr. Carrington," she managed to choke out. "Did you mention some sort of rajah? An *English* rajah?"

Carrington's frown cleared, his face brightening at this sign of her interest in his conversation. "Oh, yes, indeed. He is over there with our hostess. Would you care to take a look at him?"

Of course she would! But, then again, if it was David, would she even know it? Part of her heart wanted to turn around and run out of the ballroom, keeping her precious memories exactly as they were. The other part wanted to dash through the crowd, shouting, "Is it you? Is it you?"

She touched her ring once more, and nodded. "Yes, thank you, Mr. Carrington. I find myself—quite curious."

Mr. Carrington offered her his arm, practically leaping about in excitement at having gained her interest over Sir Arnold and Lord Pickering. "Of course, Lady

Emily! It really is most extraordinary. I expected him to be wearing a turban and ropes of pearls."

Emily slid her fingers lightly over his sleeve and followed his escort through the crowd. She smiled and nodded at the greeting of friends and acquaintances, yet did not stop to chat. There was no time for that now!

"And he was not attired thus?" she asked.

"Oh, no, not at all." Mr. Carrington seemed most disappointed. "He wore quite a nice blue coat and ivory waistcoat, surely from Weston. There was one small emerald stickpin in his cravat, but that was it. Oh, and a signet ring, but that's not Indian, is it?"

"I have no idea," Emily murmured. She tried to crane her neck to see through the crowd, but it was futile. She was just too short. And too many ladies of the *ton* favored tall plumes in their headdresses this Season.

"He was quite dark, though," Mr. Carrington continued. "And tall."

Fortunate man, Emily thought, as Lady Birtwhistle, a particularly large matron in bright orange silk, lumbered into her path.

Then, miraculously, the orange-clad lady moved aside, and there was a clear pathway between Emily and Lady Wilton and her group. Only a stretch of polished marble floor separated them.

Lady Wilton wore one of those tall headdresses, this one fashioned of purple and gold silk, with purple plumes and satin roses. She held onto an arm clad in impeccable dark blue superfine. As she laughed up at the man, her plumes waved wildly. The other three people in the cluster, Miss Wilton and Lord and Lady Hapsby, stared in wide-eyed fascination, as if they were observers at a menagerie.

As Emily took a step closer, Lady Wilton turned, and her conversation partner was revealed.

Emily could not breathe. Her skin turned cold—

freezing cold—then burned with a pink flush. Her fingers tightened convulsively on Mr. Carrington's arm.

David. It was David, here, not twenty paces away from her.

He had changed from the boy she knew all those years ago. That boy had been tall and greyhound-lean, with overlong black hair and eyes too large for his oval face. Now he was even taller, but with broad shoulders and powerful arms pulling against the expensive fabric of his coat. There was obviously no padding there, as so many "fashionable" gentlemen affected. His hair, still a shining blue-black, was impeccably cut and brushed into place, and his skin was a clear, dark olive, not burned by the Calcutta sun.

But his eyes—his eyes told her that this was indeed David. They were as dark-bright as a starry sky. Her breath caught, and she could not move.

She almost called his name aloud, but caught it the instant before it escaped. She whispered it in her mind instead. *David. David, you're back.* A ridiculous smile caught at her lips, and that she could not suppress. Her head whirled in sudden, giddy excitement.

"You see?" Mr. Carrington said cheerfully. "A real rajah, eh? Right here in London!"

Emily had a difficult time looking away from David, as if he might disappear if she turned her eyes from him. But she managed to glance up at Mr. Carrington, and gave a little nod. When she looked back to Lady Wilton's little group, her gaze collided with—David's. His lips parted a bit in surprise, and his head tilted, a lock of that hair falling over his brow like a dark question mark.

And then a smile broke across his countenance, one full of recognition and welcome. He knew her, too.

So, you are home at last, Emily thought, and she tugged at Mr. Carrington's arm to urge him forward. A crowded ballroom was not the most auspicious place for a reunion with her old friend, Emily knew that. But she did not care. She only cared that they were together again.

His first London ball. How horrid.

Before leaving England the first time, David had of course been too young for such affairs, and had rarely come to Town anyway, his father much preferring the solitude of the country. David saw now why that was so. A country assembly was much to be preferred over a grand London soiree.

Even an achingly elaborate Calcutta durbar would be preferable!

But David was an earl now. Lord Darlinghurst. He had chosen to come back to England, to take up the old duties, and this ball was the first of them. Lord and Lady Wilton had been friends of David's father, and they were kind to issue the invitation, the first (and thus far only) engraved card to arrive at David's townhouse. It was the least he could do to appear here and pay his respects to them.

He couldn't help but wish himself at home, though, where he could spend an hour with Anjali before her bedtime. They had gotten into the habit of sharing a hot pot of tea against the chill of the spring evening, while Anjali showed him her day's lessons or played him a newly learned tune at the pianoforte. She enjoyed hearing him read, too, from books of fairy tales, or poetry, or especially history. These evenings were cozy and enjoyable, quiet in the grand, if still rather dusty, drawing room.

A more different scene from the one he faced now would be hard to imagine.

David nodded at Lady Wilton's words, and made appropriately polite replies, while surreptitiously studying the ballroom. It was a vast expanse, sparkling with gilt and mirrors, yet it felt small, it was so dense with people. The dance floor was filled with skipping, swirling dancers, while its outskirts thronged with observers who talked and laughed so loudly they almost drowned out the orchestra. Their silks and muslins, their fine jewels and plumes, sparkled in the light of thousands of candles.

It put him in mind of a maharajah's audience day, when petition-seekers gathered, clad in their best garments, their diamonds and sapphires. Those people, too, whispered and watched each other, gauging where they stood in relation to their peers, if their fortunes were waning or on the rise. Were their silks finer than those of that person over there? Were their jewels larger?

David almost laughed aloud at the irony. He had journeyed halfway across the world to find that the old adage was true—the more things changed, the more they stayed the same. He had hoped that here Anjali would find a degree of freedom impossible in India, in his grandmother's world. But London was just like Calcutta in so many ways.

And he was not completely accepted in either.

In Calcutta, his grandmother's grand friends mistrusted him because of his white father, his strange Western habits. They associated him with the strange, pale sahibs. Here, they sought out his title, his English fortune, but they mistrusted his dark skin, his Indian mother. They had never met anyone like him—titled, but foreign—and did not know how to treat him.

He saw this in the sidelong glances, the half-heard whispers dragging out the old scandal of his father's marriage. People acknowledged Lady Wilton's introduction of him; he *was* the Earl of Darlinghurst, after all. But their conversation was stilted, their gazes darted above his head and to his side. He hardly dared to ask any young lady to dance, for fear their mamas would spit in his face!

It all summoned up a long-buried mischief inside of him. What would they do if he suddenly burst into Bengali, sang a song of the medieval poet Kabir, or took off his stylish coat to reveal a striped sash and curved sword? Not that he carried a sword or wore a sash, of course, but still . . . the thought was tempting. Anything to break up this stiffly artificial environment and bring some amusement.

Perhaps next time he would wear a turban. With a diamond set in it. And arrive on an elephant. Where *could* one procure an elephant in London? Or perhaps dancing girls? Yet even as he thought it, even as he was tempted to give it a try, he knew he could not. He was trying to build a new life for Anjali here, a place where she could thrive and find happiness.

But perhaps just a small elephant, in Hyde Park one afternoon. . . .

"And when will you travel to Combe Lodge, Lord Darlinghurst?" Lady Wilton asked, pulling him out of his ridiculous visions.

He smiled down at her, tilting his head to one side to avoid her bobbing purple plumes. "Very soon, I hope, Lady Wilton. I have not seen the estate in many years, and, though Town has been delightful, I am looking forward to the country air."

"Oh, yes, most bracing," said Lady Wilton, with another fervent nod that almost dislodged the plumes entirely from her headdress. "We are going to Ireland ourselves, to visit my poor sister who is forced to live there, but I do not imagine the company will be as congenial as that you'll find in Derbyshire."

"Derbyshire is a beautiful corner of the country," said Lady Hapsby timidly. She had been standing with her husband in their little circle for several moments, but this was the first time David heard her actually speak. Mostly she just clung to her husband's sleeve and stared from wide hazel eyes.

David gave her a gentle smile. "Indeed you are correct, Lady Hapsby. Some of my happiest boyhood memories are of Derbyshire and Combe Lodge. I look forward very much to returning there."

And he looked forward to seeing if the neighbors were as congenial as ever. He wondered, not for the first time, if the Kentons still resided at Fair Oak. It was a pretty place, but not as grand as most ducal seats. He remembered that it did not suit the wild Damien, but he had heard that Damien was long dead and Alex, the military younger son, was now duke. Alex was once a nice young man, who happily took David and Emily fishing and riding, when most young men could not be bothered with their little sisters and their friends. Alex, if he was still the same sort of man, would be easy to approach about selling the Star of India.

And if Emily was still in residence—well, then, the company would surely be most congenial. Unless she had become one of the stiff, formal, timid ladies he observed around him now.

That thought, the image of his pretty and energetic Boudicca turned into a porcelain doll, gave him a strange, sour pang.

"The Duke of Wayland is your neighbor, is he not?" Lord Hapsby asked, almost as if he followed David's own thoughts.

"Yes. At least, I believe the Kenton family is still in residence at Fair Oak. They were friends with my father when I was a boy," David answered. "They are a very fine family."

"Very," Lady Wilton agreed, those blasted plumes bobbing away. "The duke and duchess are meant to attend my little rout this evening, though I have not yet

seen them. I am sure they would be happy to find an old
friend here!"

"The duchess is so very stylish," her daughter, Miss
Louisa Wilton, said wistfully. "Such dash!"

"Indeed she is," agreed a nearby gentleman, and there
followed a conversation where David was informed all
about the famous, red-headed Duchess of Wayland. She
had once been Mrs. Georgina Beaumont, the well-
known Society artist, and she still occasionally displayed
her work. She drove in the park in her own phaeton, had
actually been seen embracing her children in public, and
had made dancing with one's own husband almost fashionable!

David could only hope she had not also taken to wearing the Star in her red hair and would thus be loathe to
part with it.

The talk turned to fashions in bonnets for the ladies,
and the state of hunting in Derbyshire for the gentlemen.
David had not much information, or indeed interest, in
either of those topics, and his attention drifted back to
the dancers. A schottische was finishing, the partners
skipping through the circle and swirling about one final
time.

Suddenly, the back of his neck tingled sharply, the
small hairs standing on end. Someone was watching
him, not casually, but quite intently. It felt as if he was
back in a Bengali jungle, with a panther staring at him
from the cover of trees.

Slowly, David turned away from the dance floor and
glanced behind him. His gaze landed on a lady who
stood several paces away, her hand on the arm of a
plump, red-faced young man. She was certainly
lovely—one of the most beautiful ladies in the ballroom. Not very tall, she was slim and delicate-looking,
with sunshine gold hair piled up in loose curls and an-
chored with a white silk fillet. Her gown was Grecian in

THE STAR OF INDIA

design, a simple column of white and silver satin that draped into a low décolletage and small cap sleeves. An ornate garnet cross on a gold chain hung about her neck, resting enticingly just above the swell of her ivory-rose bosom.

She would have appeared the veriest wax doll, perfectly pink and white and gold, perfectly still and polite, if not for her eyes. They were dark blue, like an Indian sky right before the onslaught of the monsoons. And they were just as stormy, roiling with a barely leashed intelligence and energy. They stared at him intently, never wavering from his face.

It was those eyes that jolted him, made him stumble back a step. Lady Wilton glanced up at him, startled. David murmured an apology to her, never taking his stare off the golden goddess.

No, not a goddess. A warrior queen. *Boudicca.*

"Emily," he whispered under his breath. It had to be Emily. No other female in the world had eyes like that. His old friend—grown into a beauty beyond all imagination.

He longed to go to her, to take her hands in his, to ask her all about the years they were separated. What had happened to her? What had she seen, done? Lady Wilton's hand on his arm held him where he was.

His hostess followed his gaze, and said, with a little trill of laughter, "Ah, here is one of your neighbors now! How fortuitous. You must remember Lady Emily Kenton." Lady Emily moved closer with her escort, a tentative smile now touching her rosey pink lips. "Lady Emily, may I have the honor of presenting, or rather *re*-presenting, the Earl of Darlinghurst? He is only recently returned from India, and has graced my humble soiree as his first outing. And this is Mr. Carrington, Lord Darlinghurst."

"Of course I remember—Lord Darlinghurst," Emily

said, her voice catching, as if she had run a great distance and was out of breath. It reminded David of the last day they were together, racing across the meadows. "It has been far too long since we met."

She stepped away from her escort, which did not please the young man—Mr. Carrington?—at all. His face grew even redder and he sputtered, but he was impotent to hold her back. She extended her gloved hand to David and he bowed over it. It was a polite salute, yet he was loath to let her go after the obeisance was performed. Her hand seemed not much larger than when he used to grasp it to help her up a tree, but her fingers were light and strong where they curled around his. She smelled of the expensive kid of her glove, of sweet roses, and of her own cinnamon-like Emily fragrance.

"Far too long, Lady Emily. It is—very good to see you again," he told her, slowly letting his hand slide from hers. She gave him a wide, glorious smile, and he was again reminded of the monsoons. She was not like a gentle English rain. Her smile, her scarcely restrained vibrant energy, were like the unspeakable relief of the cleansing, driving rains after unbearable, parching heat.

It was as if they had never been apart—and also as if they were meeting for the first time.

The orchestra tuned their instruments in preparation for a new set of dances. He thought he recognized an old country reel in the strains, a relatively simple dance he could possibly manage.

"Lady Emily, will you do me the honor of dancing the next set with me?" he asked her. He had meant not to dance this evening; his feet were still unused to the English steps, despite practicing them with Anjali for her dance lessons. His ear was unused to the tunes. Yet the chance to hold Emily's hand in his again, to converse with her, even if only in polite niceties, was more than he could resist. He could only hope he would not step on her toes, or knock her over in a turn.

Her smile widened even further, and she nodded over the sputtering, ineffectual protests of Mr. Carrington. "Thank you, Lord Darlinghurst. I would be happy to accept."

Chapter Four

*E*mily slid her hand into the warm crook of David's arm and followed his lead to their place in the dance. *Surely this must be a dream*, she thought. It felt like she was surrounded by a misty haze of unreality; her silk slippers floated above the floor, and she wanted to laugh aloud. She was about to dance with David. *David!*

She knew this was her old friend, she saw it in his eyes, heard it in his voice. Yet also, oddly, he was a stranger. A tall, handsome stranger, who had been away from her, been in a faraway land, for many years.

She wished they did not have to dance. She wanted to go somewhere quiet with him, to pour out all her questions and hear him answer in his rich, dark, musically accented voice. What was his life in India like? Why had he come back to England? Was he—unthinkable!—married? What did he think of her grown-up self?

But they could not do that, of course. They were in a crowded ballroom; everyone was watching them. Emily was accustomed to the *ton*'s eyes on her; speculation was par for the course for a duke's unmarried sister. And, of course, Georgina and Alex drew attention wherever they went in their own rights! Yet this was different. The attention seemed—sharper, somehow. The sister of the Duke of Wayland with the Indian earl? Shocking!

But Emily found she did not care. She had been through too much in her life to care two straws what the pettier members of the *ton* thought of her. As long as her actions were not dishonorable, as Damien's had been, she did mostly what she liked. And right now what she *liked* was to dance with David. There could be nothing improper in her dancing with an earl, her family's neighbor.

As she curtsied to him and took his hand for the first turn in the dance, these thoughts vanished altogether. The crowded ballroom, the other dancers, everything was gone. She saw only him, smiling at her as they came together and swirled apart. She remembered dancing with him at her parents' long-ago Christmas ball, the two of them skipping down the line, laughing as only carefree children could.

He had not been quite so tall then! His hands had not been so strong. But he still smelled of sandalwood soap.

"We were so very sorry to hear of your father's passing," she said. It seemed wrong somehow to begin their reacquaintance with such a sad subject, yet she felt it had to be said. The letter her mother had written to him when the news reached them seemed inadequate. "He was a fine man."

"Thank you, Lady Emily. I was very sorry to hear of your father, as well. And your brother." They linked arms and turned in an allemande.

He was not the best dance partner Emily had ever had; his steps were a bit uncertain, not entirely smooth. Yet he was infinitely gentle with her, not spinning her off into the hinterlands as some gentlemen were wont to do when they grew too enthusiastic. Truly, she would rather dance with David than with any other man on earth.

"Yes. Thank you. It feels such a long time since Damien left us," she answered, watching him closely. "You have been away an age."

His hand tightened on hers for the merest instant. "Much too long, I begin to think," he said.

The dance parted them, and for a while Emily could only watch him across the expanse of the set. It was not a great distance, but it felt a mile. Oh, *blast* the ridiculous rules! She wanted to *talk* to him.

When once again they came together, she asked, "And how do you find England after your years away?"

He laughed—a rich sound that made her want to laugh, too. "Cold, Lady Emily. Very cold."

She *did* laugh then. After he left, she had made it her mission to read everything she could find about India. She had been dazzled by descriptions of heat so heavy it made the very air shimmer, of strange fruits and flowers, of breezes smelling of spices.

To go from that to *this*, gray, damp, rule-bound milieu, must be shocking indeed.

"We are having an unseasonably wet spring, even for England," she said. *Weather?* She was talking of the *weather*, of all things? How ridiculous of her. "But it was quite lovely at Fair Oak the last time we were there, and it does not appear to have harmed the crops in any way. I am eager to go back to the country, as I am sure you must be to see Combe Lodge again."

"I am. I fear I have neglected it shamefully."

Emily saw a dark shutter fall over his gaze, one that spoke of worry and perhaps guilt. She understood those emotions all too well, and she hastened to reassure him. "Not at all. I ride over there often when I am at Fair Oak, and it prospers. It looks very well, the house and the fields, and I am sure you will be content when you see it."

"Thank you, Lady Emily," he said, and she fancied she heard a measure of relief. But she did so wish he could call her just *Emily* again.

"Everyone in the neighborhood will be glad you are

in residence again." She paused an instant before saying the words she was thinking, then let them all go in a rush. "Is your wife looking forward to seeing your family home? It has been many years since Combe Lodge had a mistress."

The corners of his lips twitched—whether in amusement at her presumptuous question or in a flash of pain, Emily could not tell. She did not know which option she preferred less. Why could she not call that question back? *Why?*

"I fear I am a widower," he said.

A widower! Then he was not married, and yet he had once been. What a gulf separated them since they had been apart. She wondered what other experiences he had had that she could not begin to fathom.

"I am sorry," she said simply. Inadequately.

"Thank you. My daughter is looking forward to the country, though she is as yet too young to be a proper chatelaine there. I have promised her a pony, and she talks of nothing else of late."

A daughter. And, of course, she would be beautiful, as no doubt her mother had been.

"The countryside around Combe Lodge is ideal for riding," was all Emily could think to say.

"Yes, I remember. I also remember that you were a bruising rider, who left everyone, including myself, in the dust." He gave her a teasing little smile. "Are you still so fond of riding?"

She couldn't help but smile in return, despite this new fit of self-doubt. Her rage to pepper David with questions had faded into worries that *he* would not be as interested in *her*. How could he be, when he had lived in an Indian palace with a beautiful wife and perfect, almost-pony-riding daughter? All Emily had done was run a farm, turning her hands rough and her mind hard.

"I do enjoy riding, though I do not get the chance as

often as I would like," she said, giving a little leap and a spin. "There is no place for a good gallop in Town. But my sister-in-law is teaching me to drive a phaeton. I hope to have my own very soon!"

He gazed down into her eyes as they turned, and she felt her cheeks grow warm beneath his dark regard. Oh, the curse of her pale skin, that blushes showed so clearly there! Other men looked at her all the time, and she never—ever!—blushed. She was becoming a complete ninny.

"A new chariot, Boudicca?" he asked quietly.

Hearing the old nickname in his new voice made her blush burn out of control, and she had to look away. Over David's shoulder, she saw Georgina and Alex standing at the edge of the dance floor, watching her. Alex frowned in a most fearful way, as he always did when a man he did not know spoke to his sister. But Georgina looked almost—delighted.

"One I hope does not come with blades on the wheels," Emily managed to answer, turning her attention back to her dance partner. "I should hate to frighten dogs and small children in the Park."

David laughed, and the music came to its final crescendo. Could their dance be over already? Surely it had only just begun.

Emily curtsied as David bowed, all that was correct despite the thoughts roiling in her mind. As she straightened and took his proffered arm, he said, "May I escort you to supper later, Lady Emily? If you do not already have a partner."

Did she have a partner for supper? She could scarcely recall. But then, she could scarcely recall her own name at the moment. "Thank you, Lord Darlinghurst. I would enjoy that." She turned to see Alex and Georgina moving toward them, the two of them obviously filled to the brim with filial determination. "You must allow me to present you to my brother, whom of course you already know, and my sister-in-law. They will be most eager to converse with you."

Only after the introductions had been made, and Alex and Georgina engaged David in a lively discourse about Fair Oak and Combe Lodge, did Emily have a most startling thought. Not once during their dance had she thought about the dilemma of the Star. She had been faced with a person most closely concerned with the jewel, and she herself had pondered little else for days. Yet it had completely vanished when David took her hand in his.

How strange. And how worrisome.

The Wilton dining room was almost as long as the ballroom, but it felt a great deal more intimate and less crowded thanks to the arrangements of many small, round tables rather than one long expanse which all the guests had to crowd around. Great silver platters and tureens bearing all manner of delicacies graced each table, surrounded by clusters of hothouse flowers and gold-rimmed crystal goblets of ruby red wine and sparkling champagne.

Emily was ordinarily excessively fond of baked salmon, lobster tarts, white soup, and pineapple (indeed, she knew that if she was not equally fond of exercise, she would soon be quite as large as Lady Birtwhistle in her orange satin). Yet tonight she could do no more than nibble at a few grapes. And that was due entirely to the man who sat beside her.

They were seated at a small corner table with Alex and Georgina, who asked David a myriad of questions about his plans for Combe Lodge. Emily herself managed to articulate a few comments, but mostly she just watched David—this new, fascinating David—and listened to him as he spoke.

It still felt quite unreal—dreamlike, really—that he had suddenly appeared back in her world. His smile still held echoes of the friend she had once known, but it was not as open as it had once been. His laughter held a wry, hard note under its dark music.

Well, it *had* been many years. And no one knew better than Emily the toll that time could take. Nothing stayed the same for even a moment—not even friendship. She was not the same wild, carefree girl she was then. He could not be the same boy who spent patient time with her and was her faithful friend and playmate.

She listened to him speak of his English home, and longed to ask him about other things, things she knew of only from books. Monsoons, ghats and bathing in the sacred Ganges, rajahs atop jeweled elephants, dancing girls in bright silks and belled bracelets. Did the air truly smell of spices and jasmine in India? If she leaned close enough now, could she smell its echoes in his midnight hair?

She even moved toward him, just the merest fraction, when she was brought up short by the sound of her brother speaking her name.

Emily sat up straight, and blinked innocently across the table at Alex. Surely no one looking at her could have even an inkling that she was just about to sniff a gentleman's hair!

"I beg your pardon, Alex? I fear I was examining Mrs. Harcourt's extraordinary turban and did not hear you."

"I was just telling Lord Darlinghurst that you are quite the expert on the most modern farming techniques, and he should ask your advice as well as my own concerning the fields at Combe Lodge," Alex said, with an obviously puzzled frown. Emily was not usually so concerned with such things as turbans, and she had often expressed disdain for the fashion, which of course her

brother would remember. She should have conjured up a
better excuse for her rude inattention!

Emily gave him another smile, and thought what a
very unromantic subject *farming* was compared to jasmine and spangled silks and moonlit nights in Hindu
ruins. But she *had* kept up with new farming theories,
regularly reading the agricultural reports. As much as
she longed to, she could not leave her past work behind
her entirely. Whenever she rode over Fair Oak, she
thought of planting and crop circulation. And, if all that
meant she could converse with David a bit longer, she
was glad for it.

"Indeed," she said. "While Alex was so bravely fighting for his country, I did what I could to learn about agri-
culture. The landscape and soil conditions at Combe
Lodge are, of course, very similar to those at Fair Oak. I
will be happy to share anything I have discovered."

"Thank you, Lady Emily. You are most obliging,"
David replied, giving her one of his small, wry smiles.
She noticed then the tiny lines that smile etched about
his dark eyes—lines carved there by the brilliant Indian
sun. "I have much to learn. While I read a great deal on
the voyage to England, books are no substitute for expe-
rience."

Amen to that, Emily thought. She sometimes felt that
all she had ever seen of true life was in the pages of
books. First, because books were the only amusement
she could afford while she lived alone with her mother in
the country. And now—now books were her anchor to a
different reality, in the midst of this glittering, artificial
world.

"Ah, but I hope you are not going to abandon Town
for the country just yet!" declared Georgina, with one of
her merry trills of laughter. "The Season may be almost
over, yet there are many delights still to be had. The theater, of course, is always amusing, and there is the Mer-

ryvale rout and that ridiculous affair the Innises have devised to display their treasure one last time. And you
must see the Elgin Marbles!"

Emily nodded in fervent agreement, pushing aside the
distressing mention of the forthcoming Innis ball. She
had already seen the Greek Marbles once, in their dark,
cramped display room at the British Museum, and had
been caught up by the *life* of them, the flowing, eternal
beauty. "Oh, yes, you must see at least that before you
leave London, Da—Lord Darlinghurst." She felt her
face warm anew at that near faux pas. Though she could
not *think* of him as anything but David, it would never,
ever do to say it aloud. She turned away to take a cooling sip of wine.

But he appeared not to notice her discomfiture at all.
Or perhaps he was just being polite? "Thank you, Your
Grace, Lady Emily. I would enjoy all of those things, especially the marbles, I am sure, but I do hope to leave
soon for Combe Lodge. I have my nine-year-old daughter with me, and I fear she may grow bored in Town."

"Our children are also here in Town, Lord Darlinghurst, and I know very well the importance of keeping little ones amused and out of mischief!" Georgina
said. "They are probably too young to be company for
Lady . . ." She paused, one dark red brow raised in in-
quiry.

"Lady Anjali," David answered.

Georgina nodded, not even batting an eyelash at the
exotic name. "For Lady Anjali, but perhaps she would
enjoy some of the same amusements they do, such as
Astley's Amphitheatre or some of the museums of cu-
riosities. And the Park is always most pleasant."
Georgina paused again, a speculative glance turned onto
Emily.

Emily held her breath. Whenever her sister-in-law got
that look in her eye, mischief was soon to follow.

Georgina had recently been the orchestrator of her friend Mrs. Rosalind Chase's marriage to the poet Viscount Morley, and the success had put matchmaking into her blood.

"Indeed, Lady Emily knows Hyde Park very well, she is always riding and walking there, often with my children," Georgina continued. "Perhaps she could show you—and your daughter—the best sights."

David glanced at Emily—a quick, unreadable look. She fancied she saw some uncertainty there.

But when he spoke, his voice conveyed no hint of reluctance or sense of being coerced. He smiled at her, and said, "I would be very happy if you would consent to drive with me in the Park, Lady Emily. We have many years to catch up on, after all."

"Thank you, Lord Darlinghurst," Emily answered politely, quietly, as if her stomach was *not* turning over with excitement. And all over a simple invitation to drive in the Park! "We have no engagements tomorrow afternoon."

"Excellent. Tomorrow it is," David said.

Georgina gave a satisfied little smile. "And I hope you and Lady Anjali will take tea with us next week, as well. It is always pleasant to get to know one's neighbors!"

Alex laid his hand over his wife's, and nodded in agreement. "Indeed, Darlinghurst, we will be happy to see you at any time it is convenient. And now that my wife has arranged everyone's social schedules to her liking, shall we find some fresh air on the terrace? It has grown quite close in the dining room."

"A wonderful idea, my dear!" Georgina declared. "We shall all go together."

Emily watched as Georgina and Alex rose from their chairs and ambled happily away, arm in arm, everyone moving out of the way of their ducal path. Then David's gloved hand appeared before her, waiting to help her from her seat.

She gazed up at him, and could not help but grin yet again in abject happiness. Her uncertainties about this new David, her fears about what might happen when he found out the fate of his family's Star, were pushed aside—at least for the moment. For now, for this one evening, she was just glad to see her friend again.

"Shall we join them, Lady Emily?" he asked. "I can send one of the footmen for your shawl."

She slipped her hand into his, reveling in the feel of his fingers closing over hers, holding them safe. "Thank you, Lord Darlinghurst. Some fresh air sounds most— bracing."

David studied Emily carefully in the flickering light of the Chinese lanterns strung along the Wiltons' terrace. She appeared to be everything a young English lady should be—serene, polite, charming, and oh so beautiful in her fashionable gown and jewels. Her gloved fingers were light as a butterfly on his sleeve, and her smile was perfect as she chatted with him about a myriad of incon-sequential topics—the weather, the Wiltons' elegant arrangements in their ballroom, his voyage from India and his new London townhouse.

Everything but the things he *really* wanted to ask her. What had she been doing in the years they were apart? She was obviously not engaged, but was there a young swain she favored? Above all, what was it that burned so behind her monsoon eyes, beneath the serene mask of her pretty face?

For there *was* something. He had not imagined the flare of some strange panic in her expression back in the dining room. They had been talking and laughing with her brother and his wife, when suddenly Emily's eyes widened, her breath caught in a sharp gasp, and she withdrew into some secret room deep inside herself. She dwelled in that room still, despite her smiles and polite questions.

He remembered that she would do that sometimes as a child, when she was roundly scolded by her governess or when the wicked Damien broke one of her dolls. What could be affecting her so now? She was obviously a Diamond of Society, admired and lovely. But something plagued her, something that made her go from laughing and open to quietly withdrawn in only a moment.

He would give his newly acquired phaeton to know what it was, to take the burden from her slim shoulders.

"I trust your mother is well now?" he said, trying to fill the silence between them as they turned and made another circuit of the terrace. Several feet ahead of them walked the duke and duchess, arm in arm, laughing together softly, intimately. "I understood she had an accident of some sort."

"Yes," Emily answered quietly. "Many years ago, she was thrown from her horse during a hunt. She has been confined to a Bath chair ever since."

"I am so sorry, Lady Emily," he said, chagrined. "I should not have brought up such a painful subject."

"Not at all! You and your father were always good friends to my parents—it is only natural you would want to know how she fares. And she is very well now. She is at the dower house at Fair Oak now, but she spends part of every year in Bath, taking the waters and enjoying concerts and card parties. She will be happy to hear you are back in England."

"And I am happy to hear she is doing so well." Ahead of them, he saw the duke and duchess stop and speak to another group. Soon, he and Emily would not be alone—or nearly so—any longer. He turned to her, and said quickly, "Lady Emily, shall I call on you at three o'clock to go driving with me in the Park tomorrow? I would so much like to hear more about your life."

She paused for an instant, her eyes wide and uncertain, and he feared he had pushed too much. But then she nodded, and said, "Oh, yes. I would like that very much. Thank you, Lord Darlinghurst."

Chapter Five

"*A*unt Emily, may I go driving in the Park with you, *please*?" Emily's little niece, Elizabeth Anne, caught at Emily's skirt with her chubby fingers and leaned against Emily's chair in her most beguiling manner. "It is such a beautiful day!"

Emily laid down the book she was halfheartedly reading, but before she could answer her niece's entreaties, Georgina broke in.

"No, my darling, not today," she said, barely glancing up from the sketchbook on her lap. Only her tiny, secret smile revealed that she heard all of her cajoling and was vastly amused by it. "Aunt Emily is going on a grown-up outing this afternoon. No little girls allowed. I will stay home, though, and we can have a drawing lesson."

Elizabeth Anne smoothed her palm over the sleeve of Emily's pale yellow silk walking dress. "Is that why you are so dressed up, Aunt Emily? Do you have a *suitor* coming to take you to the Park?"

Emily laughed, and caught up Elizabeth Anne's tiny hand to kiss it. "You are becoming a wild romantic, my cherub! Just like your mama. I have an old friend coming to take me to the Park, someone I knew when I was not much older than you are now."

Elizabeth Anne's brow wrinkled in confusion. *This*

did not fit into her *Cenerentola* view of life as one long vista of Prince Charmings! "A child is coming to take you driving?"

Emily could hardly contain her mirth. She pressed her hand to her mouth, and only when she felt she could speak without bursting into laughter did she say, "No, my dove. He was a child many years ago, as I was, but now he is grown up. He is as old as your mama."

Elizabeth Anne's green eyes widened. "As old as *that*?"

Emily could not help it—she let her laughter run free. "I know, angel. It is difficult to believe."

Georgina tossed a velvet cushion at Emily's head, and cried out in great indignation, "Oh, thank you *very* much, sister dear! If I only had my walking stick to hand, I would hobble my decrepit self over there and beat you soundly with it. But we elderly folk must content ourselves with our quiet seat, where we may nurse our gout."

Elizabeth Anne glanced from her mother to her aunt, obviously now thoroughly confused. "So, an *old* person is coming to call on you, Aunt Emily? *And* a child?"

"Neither, my darling," said Georgina. "Aunt Emily's caller is a most handsome gentleman of thoroughly youthful age."

"Ah." Elizabeth Anne nodded thoughtfully. "Will he bring flowers, then?"

"If he knows what is good for him. Now, leave your auntie alone for a time. You will wrinkle her gown and muss her hair."

Elizabeth Anne immediately removed her hand from the vicinity of Emily's sleeve. "Oh, no! You must not be *mussed* when your suitor comes here." She retreated to the window seat, where Georgina's white terrier, Lady Kate, was nursing her new litter of puppies. Next to clothes and fairy tales, the pups were Elizabeth Anne's first priority in her young life.

Georgina laid aside her sketchbook, and leaned over to be sure baby Sebastian still slept in his basket. "He *is* very handsome, is he not?"

"Sebastian?" Emily said, pretending to be thoroughly ignorant of Georgina's meaning. "Undoubtedly. He looks just like Alex, or shall in fifteen or twenty years."

"Of course not Sebastian! It goes without saying that *he* is handsome. And you know perfectly well who I mean. Your Lord Darlinghurst."

Emily could feel that curse of a flush returning, spreading warmly down into her ruffled white gauze chemisette. She turned away from Georgina's searching gaze, and riffled through the pages of her book. "He is not *my* Lord Darlinghurst, Georgie."

"Hm. Perhaps not yet, but judging from the way he looked at you last night, he very soon will be. Or *could* be, if you wanted him."

"Georgie! I have not seen the man for nigh on fourteen years. How should I know if I *wanted* him? We are merely two childhood friends becoming reacquainted."

"Of course, Em. But perhaps, as you become reacquainted, you will find you have things in common. Things that might lead you to—become friends again."

Emily could not pretend to herself that she had not contemplated the same sort of thing. Last night, and in the carriage coming home from the ball, and alone in her bedchamber, all she had thought about was David. How he had grown into a very handsome, fascinating man. How strong and warm his arm felt beneath her hand as they strolled along the Wiltons' terrace.

His dark eyes and rich voice, his air of something exotic and undefinable, made all her London suitors fade away into pale nothingness. But . . .

"Our lives have been so very different all these years.

Almost as if we lived on two different planets. I am sure that after the Indian ladies he would find me as dull as dishwater." As washed-out as she thought her English callers.

Georgina gave an indignant huff. "How could he possibly find you dull, Em? You have more wit and conversation that any other miss in London! Not to mention a curiosity and intelligence he could not find anyplace else, as well as your quite à la mode prettiness. I have wished all my life to change this red hair of mine into golden curls. You give yourself too little credit. Once he gets to know you again, he will be *yours*."

Emily just laughed. She could think of no reply to make, as was so often the case with Georgina's pronouncements. Emily wished that Georgina's words were true, but doubts plagued her so that she could not quite believe them. Her life *had* been very different from David's. And then there was the matter of the Star.

He would ask about it eventually, she was sure of that. The sapphire rightly belonged to him, to his family, and *her* family had done him a great wrong. She could never make the matter of the jewel right for him, no matter how much she twisted herself into knots about it. She would simply have to confess the ugly truth.

But not yet. Not until he asked. For now, she would be a selfish creature and enjoy having his company again.

"Is this him?" Elizabeth Anne cried, pressing her nose to the window. "It must be; he is stopping here. Oooh, he *is* handsome! But very dark. Do you suppose he stayed too long in the sun, Mama?"

Georgina hurried over to the window beside Elizabeth Anne, pressing her nose against the glass in the exact same manner as her small daughter. "He has been living in India, darling, and sometimes people there *are* dark. Remember the story Aunt Emily has been telling you?"

Elizabeth Anne nodded. "About the blue god with many arms?"

"Exactly. That tale also comes from India, dear."

Emily smiled at Elizabeth Anne's memory. Perhaps it was not strictly proper to read wild tales of "heathen" India to an English duke's daughter, but Elizabeth Anne loved them far above tame Anglo fables. And Emily loved reading them to her—it was good to have someone to share her interest in India with, even if it was just her little niece.

Elizabeth Anne glanced over her shoulder at Emily. "Will he know the blue man, Aunt Emily?"

"No, poppet. The blue man is made-up, remember?" Emily said.

Elizabeth Anne's face fell in comic disappointment. "Oh, yes. I remember now." Then she and her mother returned to spying out the window.

Emily took advantage of their moment of inattention to hurry over to the large gilt-framed mirror hung on the silk-papered wall. Her hair was still confined neatly within its pins, her wild yellow curls turned into a few fashionable ringlets about her face, but she fussed with it nevertheless, pushing some tendrils back, twining some about her finger. The faint, light brown freckles that sprinkled across her nose—a legacy of her seasons out in the farm fields, and now the bane of her life—had only been partially disguised by the rice powder she applied this morning.

But there was nothing to be done about that now. Greene, the butler, was already opening the drawing room door to admit their caller. She gave a final fluff to her skirts, fixed what she hoped was a welcoming and *not* maniacal smile on her face, and turned to greet David.

Georgina, always the most excellent of hostesses, hurried to the door with her elegant hand outstretched.

"Lord Darlinghurst! How very pleasant to see you again. Will you take tea before you and Lady Emily have your drive?"

"Thank you, Your Grace," David answered. "That would be most agreeable." He bowed over Georgina's hand, and tossed Emily a smile over to where she stood half-frozen by the mirror. And—was that a *wink*? Indeed it must have been!

It made Emily want to giggle like a silly schoolgirl. All of this nervous formality did seem a bit absurd. This was *David*, whom she used to race across meadows and with whom she climbed trees. But she did not yet know how she ought to behave with him. They were no longer children, but there was as yet no guide for what they should be to each other as adults.

So, for now, formal politeness it would be.

"Elizabeth Anne, dearest, ring the bell for tea," Georgina instructed her daughter, as she led David to a comfortable grouping of chairs by the fireplace. She gestured for Emily to join them.

Elizabeth Anne rang the tasseled bell pull, her wide gaze never leaving their visitor. She had one finger in the corner of her mouth, a babyish habit of which Georgina had long ago cured her, but which sometimes reappeared in moments of excitement. She came to lean against her mother's knee, and removed her finger to say, "Do you know the blue man with many arms who lives in India?"

"Elizabeth Anne!" Georgina admonished. "What did your aunt and I just tell you about that?"

"That he is a made-up man in stories," answered Elizabeth Anne, completely unabashed.

Emily gave David a sheepish smile. "I am sorry, Lord Darlinghurst. I have been reading her tales of India, and they have rather gone to her head. She was full of anticipation when she heard you had lived there."

David just laughed. "Not at all. My own daughter enjoys tales of Shiva very much. Your daughter is obviously a curious and learned girl, Your Grace."

"Indeed she is," Georgina said fondly, reaching down to smooth her child's wild red curls. She lifted Elizabeth Anne onto the seat beside her, holding her still with a firm arm about her waist. "Sometimes a bit too much so."

The tea arrived then, borne by two liveried footmen and placed carefully on a low table between Emily and Georgina. There were far too many delicacies for four people: trays of sandwiches, cakes, and tarts along with two kinds of tea. It was obvious that Cook knew Elizabeth Anne was in residence. The child had a prodigious taste for cakes second only to Emily's own.

But today Emily found her stomach was too queasy to partake of her favorite cream cakes at all.

"Lady Emily has indeed been reading Elizabeth Anne stories of India," Georgina said, pouring out the steaming tea into her best Wedgwood cups, paper thin and surrounded with pale Grecian figures. Only the most honored guests were permitted to use the Wedgwood. "She knows a great deal about the land."

David shot Emily a curious, questioning glance. "Does she truly?"

"Oh, yes! She is always telling us facts of the flora and fauna of Bengal. As an artist, of course, I have many questions about the landscape and people. Perhaps you could tell me, Lord Darlinghurst, about the grand mausoleum of the Taj Mahal? Is it as wondrous as they say?"

And Georgina went on for the next quarter hour or more, peppering David with questions about India and his life there, thus mercifully saving Emily from having to converse much herself. This gave her the chance to observe David closely as he spoke. He still smiled eas-

ily, as he had when they were younger. But there was
something different in his eyes—something mysterious
and almost sad.

But she could not really talk to him until they left the
house in David's new, stylish phaeton and turned into the
gates of Hyde Park. Aside from the people riding and
walking there, they were quite alone.

It was a bit too early in the afternoon for Rotten Row
to be truly crowded—Emily and David were actually
able to move forward in the phaeton without stopping
every ten paces or progressing at a snail's pace. Riders
cantered sedately along, ladies took the air in their open
carriages, nannies shepherded their little charges, dogs
darted about on leads, barely controlled by footmen as-
signed to their care. In the distance, Emily thought she
glimpsed Lord Pickering and Sir Arnold Ellis, on horseback paused in a small grove of trees. Sir Arnold's emerald green coat stood out like a beacon. She turned her
open yellow silk parasol toward them, so they would not
see her and come speak to her, as they always did.

She did not want anything to interfere with this moment, this illusion of solitude with David. And she was
not sure she could speak lightly and coherently with anyone—not with all the thoughts dashing around in her
head.

They had been silent as they drove away from the
house, Emily feeling the sharp stares on the back of her
neck until they turned the corner. She knew that
Georgina and Elizabeth Anne were watching avidly
from the window, and it made her want to laugh aloud.
Now that they were alone in the sunny afternoon out-
doors, she *did* laugh. It was truly ridiculous that her
glamorous sister-in-law was so very interested in
Emily's own quite dull life!

David glanced over at her, a half-smile quirked the

corner of his lips. She noticed a small dimple, and had the oddest, almost overpowering urge to place her fingertip over it and feel his smooth skin beneath her touch. Was that enticing dimple there when they were younger? How had she failed to see it then?

Ridiculous girl! she chided herself, and tightened her grip on her parasol handle until the carved ivory bit into her palm.

"Something amusing, Lady Emily?" he asked.

Emily started to retreat into her usual reserve, to give some polite, tossed-away answer. She had become quite expert at hiding her true thoughts, her fears and apprehensions and odd sense of humor, behind cool smiles and distant politeness. It was easier that way. It made her feel less apart from those around her and less like a strange creature.

And more lonely.

But this was David, she remembered. Once, she had been able to tell him anything, any fear or joy or silly joke. Just because he was now a tall, handsome, delicious-smelling man with intriguing dimples, that did not mean her friend was not still there under all that splendor. The boy who had been patient and kind with her, who had always been up for a lark or laugh, must still lurk behind his dark rajah's eyes.

She rested her parasol against her shoulder and smiled up at him. She was determined to find her friend there, and to show him that really she was not so very different, either. Surely she could still laugh, *really* laugh, even though she felt one hundred years old so much of the time. "Oh, no. I just—that is, I want to apologize for my sister-in-law's . . . nosiness. That is really the only word for it. She is an artist, you know—quite a famous one—and views every new acquaintance as a potential subject. She meant no harm by asking you so many questions about yourself and your life in India. And she is also a rather informal mother, who gives free rein to her daughter's curiosity. As, I admit, do I."

"Not at all, Lady Emily. There is no need to apologize. The duchess and Lady Elizabeth Anne are quite charming. I can see where it would be impossible *not* to indulge such a child," David said, his voice full of the deep force of his own suppressed laughter. "After so long in India, where everyone is so painfully aware of etiquette that they never say anything in the least bit unexpected, I enjoy true conversation. It is a relief."

"And so do I!" Emily exclaimed in delight. "London is surely no better than India in its formal ways. No one ever says the true, real thing—one must always guess what a person is thinking. The conversation is all weather and fashion and housekeeping and horses."

"I have noticed, in my short time here, that such topics *are* quite common. I spent at least ten minutes with Lady Wilton at her ball speculating on whether or not it would rain the next day. I would have thought the interest in such a question would wane in two minutes at the very most."

Emily laughed. "Ah, but as I recall it did *not* rain this morning. Was that the consensus you and Lady Wilton reached?"

He chuckled, and tugged at the reins to turn the horses for another circuit of the Row. "I fear I cannot recall, Lady Emily. Pray tell me, do you think we will see rain *tomorrow*?"

Emily's laughter grew louder, drawing the surprised glances of a mother and her pastel-clad daughter. Their escort, who looked suspiciously like Mr. Carrington, gave her a hurt stare, but Emily could not care. The nervous knot in her stomach was at last melting, and she began to enjoy herself. "La, Lord Darlinghurst, I could not say! But that cloud in the distance appears quite ominous. I fear it may ruin Lady Egghurst's Venetian breakfast and a planned balloon ascension."

"A Venetian breakfast? This must be a new style of event I have not heard of, Lady Emily. Pray enlighten me as to its function. Or are social events not considered one of the suitable topics for conversation?"

"On the contrary, it is the *most* suitable. Yet I fear a Venetian breakfast is not as exotic as it sounds. My brother and sister-in-law travel to Italy quite often—the duchess owns a house in Venice, and she says there is nothing at all Venetian about such soirees. They are dull affairs."

"Then I should not attend?"

"If you have a choice, no. Alas, I have no choice, as Georgina already promised, in a moment of great weakness, that we would be there. Though, if you do come, we could discuss the weather to our hearts' content."

"I shall be there, then. I cannot resist a good conversation about the rain."

There was a new note in his voice, one Emily had not heard before. It was tinged with a deepness, a seriousness—a flirtatiousness? It was hard for her to tell. Gentlemen were so awed by her brother's status that they seldom flirted with her. Emily peeked at David from beneath the brim of her bonnet, but she could see only his profile, as clear-cut and expressionless as if carved on an ancient Indian coin.

Emily decided she must have been mistaken, and she turned away to nod at a passing acquaintance. "It will be amusing if you are there. At such routs, when I grow bored, I imagine myself taking off my slippers and climbing onto the table to wade in the Roman Punch or some such outlandish deed. It would liven things up immensely, I daresay, but alas, I never have the courage!"

David laughed, and when he spoke again his tone was its usual light politeness. Yes—she had surely imagined any flirtatious admiration. She almost sighed aloud in what felt surprisingly like disappointment.

"So, you have never carried out your imaginings, Lady Emily?"

"I am no Caro Lamb. But the imagining does help to pass the time. I also sometimes make up fairy tales in my head to tell Elizabeth Anne later."

"Tales of blue men with many arms?"

Emily gave an abashed laugh. "I meant no disrespect in telling her that, I promise. But she does so enjoy stories of India, and someone gave my brother a book of Hindu tales. I thought she would like some of them, the more, er, humorous ones." Emily felt that treacherous old blush spreading again as she recalled some stories of the gods' many amorous exploits, stories she would *never* tell her niece, but which she herself quite enjoyed. She strategically turned her parasol so he could not see her red cheeks and guess her thoughts.

"My own daughter enjoys such tales," he replied. "But she also likes old stories of English kings and queens, especially Queen Elizabeth. We read many of them on our long voyage from India."

Emily frowned a bit at this reminder of the family life that had, for David, filled the years they were apart. She wondered again about his wife, his love for her. But she was not quite so willing to let go of the niceties she had just mocked, in order to ask him about those things. "How is your daughter enjoying England, now that she is here?"

He hesitated for an instant before answering. "Quite well, though I fear she has developed a taste for the bloodthirsty. We visited the Tower, and she had no interest in the jewels or the menagerie. She wanted only to see where Anne Boleyn and Catherine Howard are buried. I hope to find a proper governess for her very soon, and hopefully she can turn Anjali's interests toward more suitable avenues."

"If you are having difficulties, I am sure my sister-in-law could assist you. She has only just found a governess for Elizabeth Anne."

"Thank you. I would appreciate any advice very much."

They fell into a comfortable silence as they turned away to drive toward the Serpentine. It was growing more crowded along Rotten Row, but was quiet by the river. David drew the phaeton to a halt under the shade of a tall tree where they could watch the strolling couples and children floating their paper boats.

"You read a great deal about India, then?" David asked quietly.

Emily busied herself closing her parasol, smoothing down the folds of silk. "Yes. When we were children, I was fascinated by the tales you told me. Stories of the people and the land. I always imagined I could see it in my mind: the hot, burning sun, the sweet smell of the flowers, the strange colors. I imagined your mother was like a princess in a book, draped in silks and golden jewelry. And when you left, I wanted to know more. So, I read anything I could find about India. I talked to people who had just returned from there. I—I wanted to be able to imagine what your life was like."

Emily feared she had said too much with that last tentative admission. David was quiet beside her, and she fixed her gaze on a little boy feeding a clutch of ducks. She should never have admitted she thought of him so much when he was gone. Not when she was sure *he* had not thought of *her* in his years of marriage and family.

She felt something light against her hand, like a bird's wing or a butterfly. She stared down, startled, to see his fingers pressed over hers, atop the handle of her parasol.

It looked—*felt*—so right there, so warm and safe and unbearably exciting. She would never have imagined, even in her wildest flights of fancy, that the mere brush of a man's gloved hand could cause such a wild flutter deep in her stomach.

She slowly turned her hand to curl her fingers about his.

"I, too, wanted to know what your life was like here in England," he murmured, his face turned toward her. His cool breath stirred the small curls at her temple. "I wanted to know if you were happy—if you were still at Fair Oak, racing your horses across the fields, or if you were dancing in London. If you were married and had a new family."

"I do not," Emily whispered. "But you do."

"I do—I did. Lady Emily, Rupasri, my wife, was—"

But Emily suddenly did *not* want to hear about his wife, and she cut him off with a gesture. The love he had for his wife, a lady of his own country, a lady Emily herself could never be—how could she hear of it and not be wounded? She could not breathe; she wanted her old, safe façade back.

She slid her hand gently away from his, and gave a light, if slightly forced (even to her own ears) laugh. "La! We have known each other so long it sounds silly for you to call me Lady Emily. You must call me just Emily, and I will call you David, at least when we are alone like this. Agreed?"

He looked very much as if he wanted to say something else, something more. But finally he just nodded, and gave her a gentle, almost understanding smile, as if he could see her fears. Just as he had when they were children. She *hated* that at this moment.

"Agreed, Emily," he answered, her name coming easily from his tongue. "But I would like to tell you—"

"Lady Emily! Good afternoon!" someone called, saving her from whatever David wanted to say.

Feeling like an emotional coward, she turned to that voice in some relief—only to freeze. Sir Charles and Lady Innis were riding toward her on a pair of lovely bays, Lady Innis's stylish dark green habit and veiled hat shimmering under the late sunlight.

The Innises! Who possessed the Star of India. And Emily had *not* yet told David the sad story of the jewel. She didn't want him to hear it from strangers.

She would have to call up every ounce of polite, inane, vivacious chatter she could find to turn them from that topic.

They drew closer and closer, and Emily's mind raced. Weather? Sunny. Fashion? Yes, Lady Innis's lovely habit. Social events? The Innises' upcoming ball. No! Not that! The Star would be displayed there one last time in their house, the centerpiece of the soiree.

"Sir Charles, Lady Innis," she said, as they reined in their horses alongside the phaeton. "A lovely day, is it not?"

Luckily, the erstwhile merchant Sir Charles and his wife were so delighted to be seen conversing with a duke's sister that they happily followed wherever her conversation led. They were glad to meet David, an earl, yet showed no recognition of his name in connection to the Star, or if they did, they did not betray it. Just as they did not, and never had, betrayed the fact that they remembered buying the jewel from her impecunious brother so long ago. They merely chatted lightly about the weather, asked after Emily's family, and rode on.

It had been perhaps ten minutes' conversation, yet Emily felt as exhausted as if she had run a mile. Keeping secrets was a wearying business indeed, and one she could never seem to grow accustomed to, no matter how long she held onto it. Damien's old, shameful deed was like a heavy stone on her soul, and she longed to be rid of it.

But not at the expense of Alex and Georgina, and little Elizabeth Anne and Sebastian.

Her weariness must have shown on her face, for David turned the phaeton again toward the Park gates in the direction of home.

"The Innises are very amiable people," David commented. "Are they great friends of your family?"

"Acquaintances only. Sir Charles used to own a great many warehouses, and made a vast fortune in imports. Now he would like to become a country gentleman. He and my brother meet at Tattersall's quite often, and my sister-in-law and I see Lady Innis at the modiste. She has beautiful taste."

David chuckled. "Ah, arrivistes, then?"

"You could say that, and many people do. They love to entertain, and I am sure that you, a grand earl, will soon receive an invitation to a ball at their home." She glanced at him secretly, to see if he knew the particular ball she spoke of, if she was keeping a secret he already knew.

He did not appear to see that, however. He just gave her a small smile. "Should I accept, do you think? You must be my social adviser, Emily, in this strange new world I find myself in."

His social adviser? If only she could be. She could not even seem to organize her own life to satisfaction. "Oh, yes. I suppose you should accept."

And, she vowed, the next time they met she would tell him why that was. She would tell him everything. But not until then.

David watched Emily disappear behind the grand doors of her house, stopping at the last instant to turn and give him a smile and a farewell wave. Only then did he climb back up into his phaeton and turn toward his own townhouse.

He had been in London for weeks now, but still the streets and squares seemed foreign, unreal. Like an imaginary place in the books he had read to Anjali on their long voyage, trying to ease her transition to this new land. It seemed to have worked for her; she became very excited when she saw landmarks she recognized, and delighted in repeating the historical facts she learned. "Papa, did you know that the Battle of Hastings occurred in 1066? And Henry VIII was married *six* times?"

Her new life here was proving a bit easier than he had feared it would be, though she still pined for her young relatives and constantly asked why the cook could not learn to prepare a proper curry sauce. She loved the English clothes, and the toy shops with their extravagant dolls. But, to David, the houses and the trees, the people and the food and the language all took on a strange gray hue, an odd dreamlike-quality leached of vitality.

What had he been expecting when he came here, driven by duty and restlessness, and a desire for time to himself, far away from his mother's clamoring family? He could not even say. England was a strange land from his boyhood memories. Stranger in some ways than even the shimmering heat and color and music of India. It was a place he did not fully understand, but it was a part of him, just as Calcutta was. Perhaps the ale of England ran in his blood just as *tikka* and *lassi* did. Perhaps he had to be here now—was driven here by fate, to learn where his two halves could meet. Then he could find a sort of peace again.

As he turned his phaeton onto the square where his new townhouse sat, he remembered the strange lift of his heart when he first saw the chalk cliffs of Dover looming in the distance. He had lifted Anjali high, and told her, "See, *shona-moni*? We are home at last." And, for one soaring moment, he truly believed that.

He had that same feeling when he glanced up at the Wilton ball and saw Emily Kenton standing there. A lifting of the heart, the spirit—a feeling of homecoming. She was *not* the child-friend he left. She was a beautiful woman, an English rose of ivory and gold, with dark blue eyes that spoke of some hidden pain, a reserve, a past he knew nothing of. But he *wanted* to know. By God, but he wanted that more than he had ever wanted anything in his life.

Today, when he touched her hand beside the river and felt her draw in her breath sharply, he only wanted to pull her into his arms and hold her so close she could never escape him again. He wanted to inhale the fresh green-rose perfume that was so much a part of her very essence, to kiss her hair, her smooth cheek, her mouth, to bury his face in the curve of her neck. He wanted to tell her she could leave all her troubles, whatever they were, in his hands and be free of them forever. That she could once again be the free soul that ran laughing across country meadows.

He wanted to break through her wall of reserve and be as they once were—yet so much more.

It was utterly mad, he knew that—he felt the craziness of it in the depths of his soul, and thought that this could not be him. He was a thoughtful person, a man who always considered the impact his actions would have on his life, his status, his family. He was not a man to let passion ruin his existence, like his cousin Nikhil, who once drew a jeweled dagger on one of the governor-general's aides and had to be forcibly restrained and reminded of his duty—by David, of course.

That way led to insanity, and David wanted no part in it. He became the cool head in his family, the one who held everyone else together and maintained their status with the Anglo hierarchy in Calcutta. He did not mind; that was who he was, who he had always been. The pragmatic in a family of wild romantics, and that included his own parents.

Now, he did not feel like his steady, stern self at all. He had wanted to kiss Emily in the middle of the Park, to feel her soft lips, parting on a sigh, beneath his—to touch her, hold her.

He wanted that still. His body hummed, as tightly wound as a sitar string. The unreality of London had only increased by a hundredfold, though now the darkening sky was full of some new, strange music. It gleamed like a black pearl.

He drew up the horses in front of his house, and stared up at it as if he had never seen it before. It was identical to its neighbors, a tall expanse of pale stone with a black-painted door and dull, wrought-iron railings. It could have been anyone's house at all—except for the tiny face in one of the upstairs windows. Anjali had pulled back the stiff brocade draperies and watched for him, as she always did when he was gone. She waved merrily as she saw him, and disappeared from behind the wavy glass. She would run down the stairs and be waiting for him in the marble foyer, clamoring to hear about his day.

The sight of his daughter steadied him, made a sense of reality return to the topsy-turvy world around him. He *had* to be steady, for his child's sake. He was all she had here, her anchor in a new society. He could not afford to fly off in a passion, as his cousins did. As his father had once, eloping with a maharajah's daughter to the wailing consternation of all involved. He could not follow in his father's footsteps by grabbing a duke's sister in the middle of a public park.

But he *could* see Emily again. Could dance with her, sit beside her at the theater, maybe. He could talk to her, maybe find a way to win her trust again—to persuade her to tell him of the troubles lurking behind her lovely eyes.

For now, that would be enough.

For now.

Chapter Six

"*E*mily, will you stop that!" Georgina cried, flinging her paintbrush down onto her palette.

"What?" Emily, startled out of her daydream and back into the reality of her sister-in-law's studio, sat up straight and blinked at Georgina. Usually, she enjoyed being a model. It wasn't hard work, aside from muscles that sometimes cramped from staying in one place, and she and Georgina often chatted happily while Georgina painted. Today, though, Emily could not focus on her surroundings. She kept drifting away—back to the Park with David.

Had it been only yesterday afternoon? It felt like a hundred years ago, every minute of it filled with ridiculous yet inescapable thoughts.

Thoughts such as . . . how warm his hand had been on hers. How he smelled of sandalwood soap and clean starch as he leaned close to her. Had he been about to kiss her? Would she have truly let him, if the Innises had not appeared when they had? Was she really that improper at heart?

Oh, who was she fooling? Of course she would have let him! She had not even been aware she was in the Park any longer. They could have been all alone on the moon for all she knew. She only saw *him*, knew *him*.

What a cabbage-head she was. Anyone would have thought she was a sixteen-year-old with her first suitor, not sophisticated, in-her-third-Season Lady Emily Kenton. She had thought of nothing else when she was with David—or even when she was *not* with him, as now. She even forgot all about the Star and her plans. Until the sight of the Innises brought it all back.

"I am sorry, Georgie," she said, turning on her platform toward her sister-in-law and the easel. "What did I do wrong? Did I shift in my pose?"

"Not at all." Georgina dropped her palette onto a nearby table, amidst a jumble of paints and brushes and pots of water. "You have posed for me far too often for that! But you are meant to be Athena, gray-eyed goddess of war. You should be leading your troops forward into battle against the Trojans, resolute and martial. Athena would *not* have such a misty-eyed, daydreamlike expression on her face!"

Emily laughed ruefully, and lowered her bulky shield to the floor. She sat down on the settee, rubbing at her stiff neck as the white muslin folds of her improvised chiton settled around her. "I am truly sorry, Georgie. I suppose I am a bit distracted today. Fighting Trojans is not uppermost in my mind."

"Ah, yes. And may I venture a guess as to what *is* uppermost in your mind, Em?" Georgina gave her a sly smile. "A certain dark-eyed earl, mayhap?"

Emily turned away, letting her loose hair fall forward to shield the wretched blush she felt coming on. But she knew that Georgina would not be put off with a careless comment. Her Minerva Press–loving heart was always attuned to any hints of romance around her. Last year, in Bath, Georgina had even tried to play matchmaker with Emily's chair-bound mother and a retired colonel! "Perhaps I *am* thinking of David, just a bit. We *were* good friends once, after all, and it has been a very long time since we saw each other. It is only natural I would think about him."

"David is it now? You must have been good friends, indeed."

Blast! Emily so hoped Georgina would overlook that little slip, but of course she could not. "Did I call Lord Darlinghurst David? How shocking of me."

"You know you did. And it is not nearly as shocking as I wish you would be!" Georgina removed the paint-splashed smock covering her lavender muslin morning gown and tossed it over the easel before dropping into a chair. "You were gone a long time yesterday afternoon. Much longer than any of your previous drives in the Park, and you go at least three times a week. Now, the only difference I see between *this* drive and all those others is your escort. You must have been enjoying yourself."

There had been no time yesterday evening for Georgina to question Emily about her drive. They had had to dress for their separate outings—Georgina and Alex to the opera and Emily with friends to a musicale—and they had all returned home quite late. Her sister-in-law was obviously intent on making up for that now. Emily had to tell her *something*, or she would not know a moment's peace.

Yet, she could not tell Georgina everything. How could she, when she could not even find the words to explain it to herself? That strange elation at meeting David again, hearing his voice, seeing deep in his eyes that her friend was still there. The surprise and trepidation that she had *new* feelings when she saw him—feelings that made her throat seize shut and her stomach flutter. The gnawing guilt at keeping her secret. There was all that and more.

If there was anyone in the world who would under-stand, it was Georgina. She was a sophisticated lady, an artist and Society Diamond who was wildly, unfashionably in love with her husband. But she couldn't tell Georgina. She could not tell anyone—even if she knew what it truly was she wanted to tell. What was making her heart burst!

She gave Georgina what she hoped was a reassuring, sunny smile. "I vow to you, Georgie, there is not much to tell. You know how it is in the Park—everyone watching each other, prattling away about nonsensical things. I could scarcely speak two words together with Lord Darlinghurst, and none of it beyond the ordinary." Except when he held her hand ever so briefly. But that did not bear thinking about at the moment. "I do admit I am glad he is in England again, and I look forward to seeing him soon. That is all I can say at the moment."

"Oh, well, if that is *all* you can say at the moment, I suppose I must be content. I must say you are being terribly vexatious, Em!" Georgina's head fell back against the satin upholstery of her chair, as if so *vexed* she could no longer even sit up straight. "It is obvious we will get no work done this afternoon. Shall we go to Gunter's? Elizabeth Anne has been begging for an ice these four days at least, and I cannot put her off much longer."

Emily's interest piqued, and she left off plucking aimlessly at her corded sash. "Oh, yes! An apricot ice is always most welcome. But, please, Georgie, no more questions about Lord Darlinghurst."

"With Elizabeth Anne along? Of course not! It is shocking what big ears my little pitcher has grown. I vow she hears every word that is said in this house, then repeats them at the most inopportune moments."

"Hm," Emily murmured. "I do wonder where she inherited such a trait."

"May we have an outing today, Papa?"

"Eh?" David glanced up from his newspaper to smile at Anjali. "Did you say something, *shona-moni*?"

"I asked if we could have an outing today." Anjali spread copious amounts of marmalade on her toast. David was a bit worried about how fond she had grown of the sweet, sticky treat. "My new governess is to start lessons with me tomorrow? So, I think we should have a treat before that happens." She gave him her sweetest, most persuasive smile.

"And that jar of marmalade is not treat enough, eh?"

Anjali sighed, and rattled the spoon around in the almost-empty pot. "Marmalade is here every day, Papa. Treats are something out of the ordinary."

"Quite right. I think I could use a treat myself. Did you have something particular in mind, Anjali?"

"I would love another ice, Papa, a strawberry one from Gunter's."

"What, just an ice? No diamonds or rubies?"

Anjali giggled. "Just an ice, Papa! I am too young for diamonds and rubies."

"You, my dearest, are quite the easiest female to please whom I have ever met. Gunter's it is, then. This afternoon."

"You are the best papa in the world!" Anjali cried, clapping her sticky hands happily. "And I will play my new song on the pianoforte for you, too. I can play it with *almost* no mistakes."

"I will look forward to it. Now, you should run along and wash up. Molly will help you dress for the day."

"Yes, Papa." Anjali slid out of her chair and hurried over to kiss him on the cheek. "You won't forget— Gunter's this afternoon?"

"I will not forget," he promised.

"You don't have to go driving in the Park again?"

"Not today. Today is just yours."

Anjali nodded, seemingly satisfied, and skipped out of the breakfast room. David watched her go, thoughtfully refolding his newspaper. The pink ribbons tied in her black hair shimmered in the morning light, and she danced lightly on her little slippered toes.

Back in Calcutta, he had feared that bringing her to England might be a great mistake. She was a shy girl, one who was wary of change, and India was all she had ever known. But she seemed to enjoy the cooler environs of London, and did well with her new music lessons. It was true that she still clung closely to her father, and had not made any friends her own age from amongst the girls she met walking in the park with Molly the nursemaid. But surely that would come in time. As she became more assured of her place, she would grow more outgoing.

In the meantime, being away from the smothering attentions of her great-grandmother and female relations seemed to do her good. Not being constantly told that her entire worth to her family as a female was her ability to marry well freed her to think of other things— music, languages, art, history. And ices.

He smiled to think of the glow in her green eyes as she contemplated a trip to Gunter's for a sweet. It made him remember the same glow in another girl's eyes, many years ago.

Emily had once possessed the same sparkle and wonder that Anjali had now, yet something had changed in her. Oh, he knew that years had passed. They had grown up, and things could not stay the same. He himself had gone through such enormous changes.

But somehow he sensed that it was more than that with Emily. David tossed the newspaper onto the breakfast table and leaned back in his chair to remember their drive yesterday. At certain moments, for just an instant, he could have sworn he glimpsed the joyful Emily there. When she laughed at a child chasing a hoop, or watched, mesmerized, as a flock of birds took sudden flight over their heads, he saw the sparkle in her. The sparkle that said she could still race like the wind across the meadows.

But then a veil would drop, and her eyes would become wary and reserved again, her smile stiff, barely touching her lips. It was more than the years between them, the years that had made her a fine lady. She carried some secret burden, and he knew she would not relinquish it easily. Stubbornness was a trait that both the old *and* the new Emily shared.

Well, *he* could be stubborn, too. He was very good at solving other people's problems, and he *always* helped his friends and family. Emily Kenton was one of the best friends he had ever had. So, whether she wished it or no, he would discover what bedeviled her, and set about removing it from her life. Then the mischievous, merry Emily could shine forth again.

David resolutely pushed himself back from the table and stood to leave the breakfast room. He would begin this knight-errant mission with a visit to the florist.

"I beg your pardon, my lady, but these just came for you."

Emily paused in tying her bonnet ribbons to turn to her maid, Becky. Georgina and Elizabeth Anne were waiting downstairs to depart for Gunter's, and Emily was in a great hurry to join them, if only the slippery satin would cease knotting so! She yanked hard at them, drawing the hat from her head.

But her fit of impatience faded when she saw what Becky held.

Flowers—but not just any flowers. Emily received posies almost every day, roses and violets and sometimes lilies. But none like these—great profusions of orchids that were creamiest white at the petals' edges shading into midnight purple in the center. They were arranged in a basket, tied about with purple velvet ribbon. They were exotic and enticing, filling the chamber with rich perfume. Where had they been found, here in London?

Emily reached out for them, cradling them in her arms. They seemed almost unreal, as if they had been blown in from an exotic island, floating on ocean breezes to land in her room.

Tucked amongst the blooms was a note, yet Emily knew who they must be from even before she opened it. None of her usual suitors had the imagination for such flowers.

Lady Emily—they reminded me of you. Thank you for our drive. David

That was all it said, scrawled in a strong hand across the rich vellum. But it was enough.

She did not deserve such flowers. Or such a friend.

But she cherished them nonetheless. Her soul seemed to overflow as she buried her face in the orchids, drawing in all their sweet essence. "Oh, David," she whispered.

"Shall I put them in water for you, my lady?" Becky asked.

Emily breathed in sharply, and pulled away from the bouquet. She had quite forgotten she was not alone! She could not afford to drift so far from reality—not now.

"Thank you, Becky," Emily said, and handed back the bouquet, her fingers drifting slowly away from the satiny petals. "Is the duchess still waiting downstairs?"

"Yes, my lady. The carriage has been called."

Emily nodded, and took up her abandoned bonnet before drifting out of the room. In the foyer, Georgina was putting on her own hat in front of the mirror while Elizabeth Anne fidgeted at the foot of the stairs so that her nursemaid could hardly button her cloak for her. As soon as she saw Emily, the child broke away from the frustrated maid and dashed forward to seize her hand.

"Oh, Aunt Emily! Were those flowers for *you?*" she asked breathlessly.

"Indeed they were," Emily answered with a smile, swinging her niece into the air until she squealed with glee. "Are they not beautiful?"

"Bee-yoo-ti-ful!" Elizabeth Anne cried. "Were they from a prince? An Arabian prince?" Elizabeth Anne was reading the *Arabian Nights* with her new governess, and was now full of questions about myrrh and jeweled turbans and flying carpets.

"I would say an *Indian* prince," Georgina said, laughing. "Now, Elizabeth Anne, cease hanging on your auntie like that. You will crease her gown. The carriage is waiting." She tugged her child away, and gave Emily a wink. "I am sure Aunt Emily will tell us all about it later."

Gunter's was crowded at that hour, as it almost always was, with well-dressed hordes in search of fresh ices and delectable pastries. The tables were filled, and customers spilled out into the square to eat their treats on the benches and while strolling the pathways.

As Emily, Georgina, and Elizabeth Anne waited their turn to order, Elizabeth Anne changed her mind at least five times.

No, six. "I want strawberry, Mama. Do they have strawberry today?"

"I thought you wanted apricot, dearest," Georgina said, straightening her progeny's lopsided hair ribbon.

"Perhaps I do. What are you having, Aunt Emily?"

Emily sighed. She loved her niece dearly, truly she did, but sometimes her relentless energy was the tiniest bit wearying. As she turned to answer Elizabeth Anne, she suddenly paused, her attention captured by some new sweet-seekers just coming in the door. It was a little girl, not a great deal older than Elizabeth Anne—the most exquisite child Emily had ever seen. She was tiny, like a little doll in her white, fur-collared pelisse and pink frock, a little white fur hat perched atop her head. Long, glossy waves of black hair framed a small, pale oval face, and green eyes peeked shyly around the room. She hung back a bit, as if unsure about being suddenly in such a crowd.

Emily's heart went out to her. She understood what it was like to be watched, to be thrust into situations not of her own making.

The child reached up her hand to catch at a man's dark-gloved fingers. The gentleman bent down to speak to her, removing his hat to reveal his own luxuriant black hair, the same shade as the child's.

And suddenly Emily perfectly understood the girl's otherworldly beauty. It was *David* she was with. David who must be her father. This was the little girl he had spoken of.

Her mother must have been a great beauty, indeed.

Elizabeth Anne turned to see what had captured her aunt's attention. "Oh!" the child cried out. "That must be an Arabian princess!"

The other child's green eyes widened at this new attention, and she tensed as if she might flee. David put a reassuring hand on her shoulder and spoke softly in her ear.

Emily made her way across the room toward them, not seeing anyone watching her, not hearing Mr. Carrington calling her name from his table. She only saw David and that glorious bouquet of orchids before her eyes, and she had to speak to him.

He glanced up and saw her, and smiled in greeting, a flash of warmth leaping into his black eyes. That smile could truly have rivaled the bright afternoon, and it coaxed an answering smile from Emily.

But not from the Arabian princess. A small frown puckered her ivory brow, and she drew back against her father.

David's hand stayed on her shoulder, and that dream-like bubble around Emily burst like an overly full rain-cloud. They were a family, these two, and she was an outsider. Always an outsider.

She did not want to show any discomfiture, though. She kept her smile firmly in place, and said in her most polite voice, "Good afternoon, Lord Darlinghurst. It is nice to see you again."

"And you, Lady Emily," he answered, equally polite. But there was still that smile in his voice. "You are look-ing lovely, as always."

"Thank you, Lord Darlinghurst. I fear not nearly as lovely as this young lady, though. Your daughter, I pre-sume?"

"Indeed. Lady Emily Kenton, may I present Lady An-jali Huntington."

His hand gently urged the girl forward, and she took one small step. Her gaze on the floor, she dropped to give a dainty little curtsy. "How do you do, Lady Emily."

"How do *you* do, Lady Anjali." Emily was not certain what else she could say. The only other little girl she knew anything about was Elizabeth Anne, and her mis-chievous niece was nothing like this porcelain doll. This Arabian princess. But, somehow, Emily desperately wanted this girl to like her. Or at least look at her. "That is a very pretty name—Anjali. So much finer than dull old Emily."

Lady Anjali just stared back at her with wide, doubt-ing eyes. Emily found herself more tongue-tied than she had been when presented to Queen Charlotte. What did one *say* to a silent Arabian princess child?

Fortunately, before she could start babbling about how very much she hated the name Emily, Georgina and Elizabeth Anne appeared at her side, ices in hand.

"Good afternoon, Lord Darlinghurst," Georgina said. "So very good to see you again! And this must be your lovely daughter."

"Do you have a flying carpet?" Elizabeth Anne asked Anjali, her chin already sticky with strawberry ice.

Anjali's startled gaze turned from Emily to the other child. "I—no, I'm sorry, I fear none of my carpets fly."

"Elizabeth Anne! Now, what did I just tell you?" Georgina admonished, taking her daughter's hand in hers. "I am sorry, Lord Darlinghurst. I fear my child has not yet finished learning her manners."

"That is quite all right, Your Grace," David answered, with a smile just for Elizabeth Anne.

"We should take our ices out into the square, if you would care to join us," Georgina said. "Indeed, if Lady Anjali likes, she could wait with us while you order your own treats. It is a fine day, and I promise that Lady Mischief here will hold her tongue."

Emily watched as Lady Anjali's stare darted to her father's face, and her hand tightened on his. David gave it a reassuring squeeze, and nodded to her. Emily had never before seen a man behave so toward his child— not even Alex, who was utterly devoted to Elizabeth Anne and Sebastian. It was almost as if David and his daughter were an insulated world of two, where words were unnecessary for communication.

How could another person ever fit into such a world?

"Thank you, Your Grace," David answered. "I am sure Anjali would enjoy that. She was quite enthralled by a man with a music-playing monkey we saw as we were coming in. And I will be out in only a few moments with our ices. Perhaps Lady Emily will be so good as to advise me on the choice of flavors?"

"Of course, Lord Darlinghurst," Emily answered. She watched as Georgina led the children out the door, Elizabeth Anne still chattering on and Anjali looking like a startled little gazelle. David held his arm out to Emily, and she slid her gloved hand over his soft wool sleeve and walked with him back into the sugar-scented depths of the shop.

His arm was strong and steady beneath her touch, holding her up in this suddenly hazy scene.

"Your daughter is very pretty," she said, pretending to examine the array of pastries displayed before her.

"Thank you," he answered. "I, of course, would never dispute that. She is rather shy, though, and still a bit unsure of her new home."

"Of course she is. Why, I remember the first time I visited London as a child. I thought it wild and a bit frightening, like some strange world in a book. And I was just coming from a country estate, not India! She must be terribly bewildered."

"I think she was, at first, and she missed her relatives. But she is adjusting. She has enjoyed visiting the Tower, and taking a boat ride on the Thames."

"And these activities have inspired her taste for bloodthirsty history? Anne Boleyn and such?"

"Precisely! She is always full of questions about the poor queens of Henry VIII—questions I fear I am ill-equipped to answer. I know precious little about any of those ladies."

Emily laughed. "It is fortunate she met my sister-in-law, then! The duchess is planning a grand painting of the trial of Anne Boleyn, and will be able to answer any questions your daughter may have."

They took their newly made ices—lemon for David and Anjali and apricot for Emily—and carried them out to the sun-washed square. Emily blinked in the sudden rush of light after the dim indoors, and shielded her eyes with her hand to see Georgina sitting on a bench with the two girls. Elizabeth Anne was still chattering away, and Anjali sat with daintily folded hands and ankles, her pretty face carefully expressionless.

They had not seen Emily and David yet, and, for an instant, Emily was tempted to clutch at his arm, to hold him where he was. They could be alone there, in the shadow of Gunter's, for a moment, with no families or painfully polite conversation to catch them.

He must have guessed something of her thoughts, for he turned to stare down at her, his expression shaded by the brim of his hat.

"Is something amiss?" he asked quietly.

"I—no, of course not. Not at all. I just—the light . . ." Emily faltered, not at all sure of what she wanted to say.

But he knew. Just as he had always known. "I want to talk to you, too, Emily," he said, his voice still soft, as if the hurrying masses around them could hear and spoil their moment. "*Truly* talk, not this polite nonsense. Is that what you want, too? If not, just scream at me, slap my face, and I will leave you alone."

Emily had to laugh at the image of her screeching and slapping his face, causing a scene right outside Gunter's. As if she ever could! His face was too handsome to mar with red handprints. In fact, what she really wanted more than anything was to place the tip of her finger right on that enticing dimple . . .

Blast! Emily turned her stare away from him, curling her gloved fingers hard around her container of ice. The chill was a fine reminder of the reality of their situation.

"I *do* want to talk to you," she said. "Very much." But now was hardly the time. Georgina had seen them and was waving. "I am going to the British Museum tomorrow afternoon—alone, because Georgina has a meeting of her artists' salon. If you would somehow—by coincidence, of course—appear in the Elgin Marbles room by two o'clock. . . ."

He gave her a conspiring smile. "Say no more, Lady Emily. I will be there."

Emily nodded, and started across the square toward Georgina and the children. Her attention was caught by the image of a lady leaving her grand townhouse across the square—a lady in an elegant mulberry-colored carriage gown and feathered bonnet. She paused to say a word to a footman, drawing on her gloves.

Lady Innis, going out of the house where they were meant to attend a ball next week. A ball to view the Star of India before it was given to the Mercer Museum.

Emily gasped at this cold reminder of reality—a reality that came around to slap her in the face whenever she dared to enjoy a moment in the sun with David.

A reality that would soon have to be faced, once and for all.

Chapter Seven

The jeweler's shop was silent and dim as Emily slipped inside the door. At first glance, it would not look terribly promising to shoppers accustomed to the elegance of Bond Street. There were no gleaming chandeliers or enticing window displays, no velvet-upholstered settees or well-dressed attendants offering refreshments. Only if one peered closer, into the slightly dusty glass cases, was its true worth revealed.

Mr. Jervis's shop carried only the most original, the most breathtaking designs. His workers came from Paris and Venice, refugees from the harsh Napoleonic years, and their necklaces and bracelets had a cunning and an elegant lightness many of the wares of the larger shops failed to possess.

Emily had found it when she was helping her brother look for a special anniversary gift for his wife. Georgina loved jewels, but she was not a lady whose tastes ran to the conventional; the emerald and ruby inlaid cuff bracelets Alex found here suited her perfectly. Emily came back whenever she was in need of an unusual item—or when she was in trouble, as now.

Mr. Jervis's prices were very reasonable, and it was not likely that anyone of her Mayfair acquaintance would be here in Gracechurch Street to see her. Mr.

Jervis was also very willing to barter with her, taking her birthday necklace and earrings in exchange for making a perfect—and authentic—copy of the Star of India.

Her opening the door set off a small, tinkling bell, and summoned Mr. Jervis from the back rooms. He blinked at her from behind his spectacles, obviously unable to recognize her in the dim light. Emily pushed the veil of her bonnet back, and a smile broke across his thin face.

"Ah, Lady Emily!" he said. "You are very prompt."

"Your letter *did* say it would be ready today, Mr. Jervis," Emily answered, advancing into the shadowed depths of the shop. Gold and silver, diamonds and porcelain, beckoned to her from the cases, but she did not give in to their siren song.

"Oh, yes, indeed it is! I am sure you will be most happy with it, Lady Emily—it is my very finest work to date, I do declare." He ducked back behind a counter and, after some jangling and crashing noises, emerged with a small black velvet box. "Though I must say it was not easy working only from sketches."

Emily touched the tip of her tongue to her suddenly dry lips. She had not been so very nervous to enter a shop since the days of Damien's debts to every merchant in the village. But this would soon be over. "I do apologize for my poor artistic skills, Mr. Jervis. I am sure you did a superb job, as you always do."

Mr. Jervis nodded agreeably, and pressed the box open. Emily leaned over to see it better—and gave a small gasp.

It was indeed beautiful work, the oblong sapphire surrounded by smaller diamonds. It shimmered like the very sky. Emily herself could not have told it apart from the real Star—except for some elusive *something* the facsimile lacked. When she had held the true Star in her hand all those years ago, it had warmed and tingled on her palm, whispering of far-off lands and doomed love.

This jewel only whispered of cold beauty.

But no one else would ever know that. And the jewel in the Innis mansion was *not* the real Star, after all. It was just paste. The real Star was . . . no one knew where. At least this way the Innises' experts would find a genuine sapphire when they examined it.

"It is exquisite, Mr. Jervis," she said. "You are an absolute artist."

Mr. Jervis beamed. "Thank you, Lady Emily! You do have quite the eye. As you see here, I turned the facets just so, in the Indian manner . . ."

It was the better part of a half-hour before Emily could leave the shop, with Mr. Jervis's assurances he would not say anything to her brother or sister-in-law if he should see them again and the new Star tucked into her reticule. She stepped out into the sunlight, breathing deeply of the fresh air.

Oh, this was all so maddening! She was not cut out for intrigue at all. Her hands were shaking and her mouth was dry, just from traveling to the shop today. At least it was nearly over. Or it would be after the Innis ball, where she would have to find a way to exchange the paste sapphire for the genuine one.

How she would do *that*, she had no idea. Not yet.

"You are a complete widgeon at this, Emily Kenton," she muttered to herself, looping her reticule ribbons securely over her wrist. "You would have made a terrible spy in France!"

She had to return home now, and have a quick luncheon and change her gown before meeting David at the museum. . . .

David! At the thought of him, her hands shook all over again. Meeting him by the Elgin Marbles would be at least as frightening as coming to this shop this morning. Probably much more so. Somehow, every time she saw him, he grew more handsome, his dark eyes more enticing. They watched her as if they could see her soul, all her secrets. They beckoned to her to tell him everything.

But she could not do that. This was *her* burden, hers alone. David would surely hate her if he knew she had allowed her brother to sell the Star and then accepted gifts of the ill-gotten gains. Then the warmth of his gaze would turn to ice.

Emily could never bear that.

She stepped to the pavement to look for the hansom that was meant to be waiting for her—and froze. A dark blue carriage with a familiar crest painted on the door— the Darlinghurst crest—came around the corner and drove slowly past her.

David—*here!* How could that be? It was as if her thoughts of him summoned him in the flesh, right at the worst moment.

She shrank back into the shadows of the building, reaching up to snatch her veil down. But it was too late. From the half-open carriage window floated a sweet, childish voice.

"Papa! Isn't that the yellow-haired lady we met at Gunter's?"

David had thought this morning would be a good time to find gifts to send back to Calcutta for his grandmother and female cousins. Lengths of pale English muslins, with their light colors and dainty prints, would amuse them, and Lady Wilton had suggested this warehouse to him. She had given him the address in a whisper, as if it was a great secret. And, of course, Anjali had insisted on accompanying him.

As he settled her into the carriage, with the window half-open so she would not become ill from the lurching, swaying motion, he told her, "Now, we cannot be long at the shops. I have an appointment I must keep this afternoon." A very important appointment indeed, with Emily at the British Museum. He could feel himself grinning like a fool just thinking about seeing her again.

Anjali leaned forward, and said, in her solemn voice, "Is it an appointment with that lady we met in Gunter's? The one with the yellow curls?"

David stared at his daughter in surprise. He had thought she barely took notice of meeting Emily at Gunter's, she had been so very quiet. Even when they returned home, she retreated into the silence of a book. He certainly had not told her of this planned meeting. Anjali watched him closely with her large green eyes, as he concealed his surprise behind a light smile. He reached out to tweak at her hair ribbon.

"Do you mean Lady Emily, *shona-moni*?" he said carelessly. "I may see her there."

Anjali nodded slowly, her gaze never leaving his face. She looked so much like her great-grandmother when she was in such a mood, stern and all-seeing. At such times, he could hardly fathom that he had fathered such an otherworldly little creature. "Lady Emily is very pretty," she said. "But she is not very much like Mama."

That was certainly very true. Rupasri had been lovely, with her fall of black hair and smooth, honey-colored skin, but she had been quiet, submissive as she had been taught to be. She had no secrets behind her dark eyes, as Emily held in the sky color of hers. Rupasri did not seem to spring as she walked, the way Emily did. Emily seemed almost as if she would break into a dash every time she moved, as if she danced even while standing still. The power of the sun almost burst from her bright hair, from her very fingertips.

But how could he say such things to his daughter? How would she understand how Emily made him feel, when he did not even understand it himself? He only knew that when he saw Emily he felt alive.

"No," he told Anjali. "She is not very much like your mama. But she *is* very pretty, and very nice, too."

"Are you going to marry her, then, Papa?"

Anjali's quiet question conjured a sudden image in his mind—himself and Emily emerging from a church door, wreathed in smiles and rose petals. Emily turned to glance up at him, a lace veil falling back from her face as her mouth lifted for his kiss . . .

And it struck him like a crash of monsoon lightning— that was exactly what he wanted. To have Emily in his life forever, to hold onto all that life and energy and laughter and mystery. It was what he wanted the instant he saw her in that ballroom, standing there in her white gown, his old friend all grown up and beautiful.

But what did *she* want? She seemed happy to see him again; she had even almost kissed him in the park, her lips trembling with a need that echoed his own. Yet there were those secrets she held in her eyes, there was *something* that was not letting her embrace him fully. He would give his fortune to know what it was. Another love—a secret one? A gambling addiction, the same as that which had landed her oldest brother in the soup so often? Was she a jewel thief, a duelist, a French spy? . . .

The list could go on and on, growing ever more absurd. He could not think of it now. Anjali was still watching him, and he had to answer her.

He knew one thing for certain, though—whatever Emily was hiding, it could not be ugly or sinful. His friend had always shone with a pure honesty, and bright souls such as hers did not tarnish.

"Do you remember what I told you in Calcutta, Anjali?" he said. "About when I marry again?"

Anjali nodded. "That you would not marry a lady unless she would be a good mama."

"Exactly. You know I would never bring someone

into our home who would not care for both of us. Do you trust me when I say that?"

"Of course, Papa."

"Then you have no need to worry."

"So, you *are* going to marry her? The Lady Emily from Gunter's?"

David laughed. Yes, Anjali *was* like her great-grandmother—she would never let go of an idea when it was firmly in her head. "*Shona-moni*, Lady Emily and I are old friends who are becoming reacquainted. I do not know what may happen in the future, but I promise you all will be well. Yes?"

Anjali nodded, apparently satisfied—for now. She sat back against the tufted velvet cushions and watched the city scenery change outside the window. As they turned onto the street where the suggested warehouse resided, she suddenly sat straight up, pointing excitedly in direct opposition to all her etiquette lessons.

"Papa!" she cried. "Isn't that the yellow-haired lady we met at Gunter's? Lady Emily?"

"It cannot be," David said, leaning forward to peer out the window himself. His heart gave a small leap of excitement to hear Emily's name, but surely it was not her whom Anjali saw now. Whatever would she be doing in this part of Town? Anjali probably just imagined it, since they had been speaking of Emily only moments before.

Yet it *was* her, standing there on the pavement, staring at their carriage with wide, shocked eyes. She wore a plain, dark blue pelisse and a black bonnet with a veil pushed back, her hand reached up as if to draw it down. Not exactly à la mode, but it was undoubtedly her, with her golden curls blowing loose from under that bonnet, pulled by the breeze.

"By Jove, but you are quite right, Anjali," he said. "It is indeed Lady Emily."

"It is a *sign*," Anjali murmured, clasping her small hands under her chin.

David heard her odd words, yet had no time to question her as he called out to the coachman to halt. He did not wait for the footman, but pushed open the door himself and jumped out.

"Lady Emily," he called, raising his hat to her. "You are the last person I would have expected to see here this morning."

Emily threw a quick glance back over her shoulder, as if seeking some escape. She found only a hansom, and a shop whose faded sign read L. JERVIS, JEWELER. Her gloved hands clutched at her reticule. For one instant, he feared she might dash away from him.

More secrets, then?

But she turned back to him, her shoulders straightening, and gave him a bright, polite smile. She stepped toward him, her hand held out.

"I might say the same about you, Lord Darlinghurst," she answered, as he bowed over her fingers. The tips of her dark gloves were dusty. "I was just here at the jeweler, running an errand for—for my sister-in-law. It is an unfashionable part of Town, I know, but Mr. Jervis has the finest jewels."

"I shall have to remember that, then," he answered, smiling at her as he slowly, very slowly, released her hand. She folded her fingers around the reticule again. "Lady Wilton recommended a warehouse here where I might find excellent gifts to send back to my relations in Calcutta."

"Oh, yes! Of course," Emily replied, still with that too-bright tone in her voice. "Well, you must be in a great hurry to get there. I will just leave you to it, and perhaps we will meet later, at the museum . . ."

David's gaze slid past her to the hansom, where the

driver sat watching them with bored disinterest. "Never say you came here in a hansom, Lady Emily!"

Emily glanced back, as if she had quite forgotten the vehicle was there. "Oh! Well—yes. I did not want to bother with calling for our carriage."

A duke's sister did not want to call for her carriage? Curious. David watched Emily's flushed face with a little frown. Something was quite amiss here, something Emily was trying her hardest to hide. But she was a terrible actress.

And David was good at discovering secrets. He had to be, with his wild-blooded family. Just give him time . . .

"Well, you simply cannot go home in a hansom," he told her. "Please, allow us to take you in our carriage."

"Oh, no, I could not . . ." she began in a rush—then paused, a puzzled frown creasing her brow. "Us, Lord Darlinghurst?"

"Anjali and myself, of course." He smiled down at her. "You did not think I would ask you to come with me unchaperoned, do you?"

As he spoke, Anjali poked her head out the carriage window. Unlike the quiet, solemn girl she had been all morning, she was smiling widely, her green eyes sparkling like spring meadows. She waved merrily, and called out, "Lady Emily! How grand to see you again. We are going shopping for a gift for my great-grandmother. Won't you join us?"

David stared at his daughter, dumbfounded. Was there something in the air in this part of Town that made females as changeable as clouds? This was a great change since only yesterday. What could have caused it?

Emily smiled at Anjali, her frown clearing entirely for the first time since their unexpected meeting. "Good day, Lady Anjali! It is good to see you again, too. I am not certain—"

"Please, do join us, Lady Emily," David said. "Unless

you have another appointment. I confess I am quite hopeless at choosing gifts, and I would very much appreciate your opinion."

Emily looked again to the hansom, the jeweler's window, and David's carriage before saying slowly, "Very well, Lord Darlinghurst. I would be happy to join you and Lady Anjali."

"Excellent, Lady Emily. Thank you," David said, offering his arm to escort her to the carriage.

She securely tucked her reticule against her side before sliding her fingers over his sleeve. Yes, indeed, she was carrying a secret in her heart, if not in that blasted reticule itself.

And David intended to find out what it was.

Chapter Eight

*A*njali peeked out from between two tall displays of bolts of fabric, trying to watch her father and Lady Emily without them seeing her. Not that they were paying a great deal of attention to anything around them—they stood on either side of a table spread with silks and muslins, leaning in to speak together in quiet voices. Lady Emily ran her gloved hand over a length of dark green velvet, a tiny half-smile playing about her lips.

Anjali gave a decisive nod. It was as she thought. Her papa *liked* the bright-haired Lady Emily, in the way that grown-up men sometimes liked grown-up ladies. Anjali might be only nine years old, but she knew these things. Whenever she visited her great-grandmother's zenana, the ladies there would often forget Anjali was listening and would chatter on about romances and new marriages and babies. A girl could learn a lot that way—even a girl with no mother.

Her papa had never paid any attention to the dark-eyed ladies in Calcutta, or to the pale daughters of the English families who invited him to dine or play cards. So Anjali had never really paid heed to the gossip, mostly heard from her great-grandmother's lips, that said he should marry again. Their lives were fine just as they were.

She paid no heed—until she saw that Lady Emily in Gunter's, all white and gold like some ice princess in a storybook. Until she saw the way her father stared at Lady Emily, as if all else had vanished around him. He smiled when he took her hand in a way Anjali had never noticed before.

And she had felt sick to her stomach, as if she had eaten too many sweets. This lady, this—this *English* lady would ruin everything! All their cozy life of Papa taking her for drives, listening to her music lessons, taking breakfast with her—it would all end if he married Lady Emily. English children were banished to the nursery, so she had heard. Cut off from the grown-up life of the house. The thought of it made even the sweet ice taste like dust in her mouth.

It had not helped matters at all that she'd had to spend the afternoon listening to the babblings of that toddler Lady Elizabeth Anne Kenton, either!

So, that night, alone in her bed, Anjali had prayed. She considered these prayers very carefully. At first, she wanted simply to ask for Lady Emily to go away. But she knew that would not be right—God's will had to be done, and not her own. That was what her nursemaid said. If Lady Emily was truly meant to be her new mama, if it was part of the grand design for all things, then so be it.

She asked then for a sign. A sign that all was proceeding as it should, that everything would be well even if Lady Emily came into their lives.

And, surely, finding Lady Emily here, as if waiting for them in this most unlikely spot, was a sign!

And the smile on her papa's face was another. Anjali peeked over the fabrics to see him laugh at something Lady Emily said, his face brighter than the Calcutta sun. Anyone that could make her papa look like that, when he had been so serious and intent for so long, could not be all bad.

"A sign," Anjali whispered. A sign that Lady Emily was *meant* to be her mama, no matter what. Her great-grandmother always said humans must take notice when the gods chose to reveal their courses.

"It was fortuitous to meet you like this, Lady Emily," David said. "I thought fine English ladies did not deign to leave their houses until two o'clock at the earliest!"

Emily laughed. She couldn't help it—despite her trepidation at being here with him, and her panic at being nearly caught at Mr. Jervis's shop, she felt strangely light and giddy. As if she had been imbibing champagne! Even the weight of the stone in her reticule felt lighter.

"Usually I do not," she answered. "It is hard to be an early riser when one has not even returned home until dawn."

"What made today an exception?"

Emily glanced down at the figured muslin she was fingering. She found she just could not meet his open, honest gaze for a second longer. "I—had that errand to perform. I wanted to finish it before I went to the museum this afternoon. Should we find Lady Anjali? I have not seen her for several minutes."

David gave a wry smile, a quirk of his lips that told her he was fully aware of her evasions. He always had been, even when they were children—she could never lie to him. Back then, she had thought it was due to some exotic Eastern mysticism, inborn in the blood of his mother. Later, she laughed at her childhood fancies.

Now she thought she had not been so very wrong in that supposition.

David could tell that she was hiding something. She saw it in the way he watched her.

Just tell him, a little voice in her mind whispered. *He has a right to know.*

No! she argued back. *It has been so many years since we last met. How can I know if I can trust him?*

David at last looked away from her, turning his attention to the bolt of muslin and releasing her from the unbearable tension. Only as her breath escaped in a great exhale did she realize she had been holding it.

"Anjali is fine," he said. "I saw one of the shopgirls bringing her a cup of tea just a moment ago. She will have all the gifts chosen in a very short time, I'm sure. She was so excited about sending our relatives objects from England."

Just a short time. A short time to be alone with David. Emily studied him closely: the strong line of his jaw, the smooth wave of his glossy dark hair over his brow, the elegant gloved hands that lay so near her own atop the fabric.

You can trust him, that insidious voice whispered. *What choice do you have? You must trust someone.*

That was assuredly true. She could not go on all alone with this secret—the weight of it was nigh to crushing her. And David had been her best friend, could still be, if she could just quell the urge to kiss him whenever he drew near!

"David," she said quickly, before her courage could flee. "There is something I must tell you—"

"Papa! Look at what I have found. Would not *Didu* like it?" Anjali's light, childish voice called, drowning out Emily's whisper.

But, as quiet as she had been, David heard her. His hand covered hers briefly, warmly, beneath a fold of the cloth, and he murmured, "Tell me later. At the museum. There is something I must speak to you about, as well, Emily. To do with a certain trinket my father left with your family."

A certain trinket. So, he *did* remember. Emily had begun to wonder. Hope? She nodded, and his hand drew away, leaving her skin strangely chilled. She took a deep, steadying breath, and pasted on a welcoming smile before turning to the child.

Much to her shock, David's Arabian princess daughter walked right up to her and held out a length of silk for her inspection.

Emily could have vowed on their meeting at Gunter's that Lady Anjali did not care for her. She had watched Emily with wide, wary green eyes, silent and observant, as judgmental as an Almack's patroness. All of Emily's attempts at conversation were met with a polite "Yes, Lady Emily," or "No, Lady Emily."

Now, she gave Emily a bright smile. "Your own clothes are so pretty, Lady Emily, that I know you will be able to say whether it is fashionable or not. My great-grandmother will want only the very latest styles."

Emily could not help but smile back at her; the girl's open, pretty face had the attraction of sunlight on a cold, gray day. She obviously possessed her father's easy charm, when she chose to display it.

Emily knelt down beside Anjali to examine the silk. She longed to kiss the child's pretty cheek in absurd gratitude for her sudden show of friendship—and for postponing the inevitable conversation Emily must have with Anjali's father.

"It is very lovely, Lady Anjali," she answered. "This blue is very à la mode this Season. I am sure your great-grandmother could make a fine gown or pelisse from it."

"She would not make a gown or pelisse, Lady Emily. She will make a sari," said Anjali.

"A sari? My, that sounds terribly grand. What does one look like, pray tell?" Emily asked, as if she had never seen so much as a sketch of an Indian lady in her costume before. She had even tried to make one herself, from a length of pink satin, to no avail. The intricate folds were beyond her skills.

But she liked hearing the little girl speak, her tones lilting and sweet. And the solemn expression on Anjali's face as she proceeded to explain the garment was priceless.

Before the horrified gaze of the shopgirl, Anjali unrolled the entire bolt and proceeded to wind the cloth around herself. "First, Lady Emily, you must hold it like this, and turn like this . . ."

Later, when the fabric used for Anjali's sari had been put back on its bolt and the chosen purchases were being wrapped, Emily walked with Anjali among a display for hat trimmings of feathers and flowers. She stopped to examine a basket of silk roses, wondering how a yellow blossom would look on a new white bonnet.

"Lady Emily?" Anjali said softly, leaning against her ever so slightly.

Emily smiled down at her. "Yes, Lady Anjali?"

"You knew my father when you were children?"

"Yes, I did. Many years ago."

The child's pretty green eyes shifted away, as if she was uncertain about something. "Was he—happy here in England? Then?"

Emily thought she understood. After all, she had once been an uncertain child herself. She knelt down beside Anjali, her skirts spreading about her on the wooden floor. "Is there something troubling you about your papa, my dear?"

Anjali shook her head. "It is just that—he seemed unhappy while we were in Calcutta, even though he always laughed and smiled with me. I hoped he would be happy here, maybe like when you were children."

Emily felt such a sharp pang at the thought of David *ever* being unhappy about anything at all, and that it would cause such worry in this child's wide green eyes. "I hope he will be happy here. And you, too. Your papa tells me you enjoy English history, and seeing all the sights here."

"I do enjoy that. But it is not as sunny here as it is in India, and . . ." Her soft voice trailed away.

"But, what?" Emily reached out to clasp Anjali's small hand in hers. "What is amiss, my dear?"

Anjali stared at her intently, her brow wrinkled. "I see the way some people look at me when Papa takes me out, as if I was—strange, odd. My hair is dark, not like yours. Is something wrong with me? With Papa? Is that why he is unhappy?"

Emily's stomach cramped with a sudden, fiery bolt of anger that someone—anyone—could so much as look sideways at this sweet girl. Unable to stop herself, she put her arms around Anjali and drew her close. At first, the child held herself stiff, uncertain. But then she melted against Emily, her arms going about her neck. "Lady Anjali, it is true that there are some foolish people who believe everyone should look and think alike. But you must pay them no attention at all, for they are mistaken. You should pity them for being so stupid."

Anjali giggled against Emily's shoulder. "Stupid, Lady Emily?"

"Yes. Stupid. For you are perfectly beautiful just as you are, and you must always remember that. If anyone says differently, I will jab them with my parasol."

Anjali laughed again, the sound sweet as springtime birdsong. Her small hands tightened around Emily—and Emily felt her own heart laugh in light reply.

Chapter Nine

*T*he British Museum was quiet in the afternoon—so quiet that the soles of Emily's half-boots echoed hollowly on the floor as she moved between the graceful arcs of the pale marble statues, the long stretches of the friezes. That last time she had come here, with Georgina and Alex to see the new rooms for the Elgin Marbles, the crowds had been so thick she could scarcely see without trodding on someone's foot. But at this hour everyone was at the Park, seeing and being seen along Rotten Row. Only a few people, artists with sketchbooks or seekers of beauty and solitude like herself, wandered in the dim spaces like flitting ghosts.

Even with those masses pressing around her on that last visit, Emily had adored these sculptures. The graceful flow of the carvings, as if they were made of silk and muslin—warm flesh, rather than chilled marble. The transcendence of the twisting, reaching figures beckoned to her. When she gazed at them, or even reached out to touch them with the very tips of her fingers, they told her that there *was* beauty in the world. There was truth and grace, and a life to be had beyond the superficial meanderings of London Society.

She saw that same revelation in David Huntington's dark eyes, in the tender way he spoke to his little daughter, the way his laughter echoed with warmth and humor. His life could not have been easy, caught between two worlds, two vastly different cultures and ways of life, yet there seemed no bitterness in him, as she had in herself. The way he looked at Emily, the way he touched her hand, as if she was some priceless, lovely piece of porcelain, coaxed her to be honest with him, to let go of her own anger and move into a future of endless possibility.

She wished, more than anything, that she *could* do that. She was weary of carrying that hard, cold stone in her heart, a stone made out of anger toward her long-dead brother and her own guilt. If she could, she would drop it right now, leave it at the feet of this statue of Hestia, and never look back.

Yet how could she when Damien's actions of so long ago, her own actions, were forcing her now to tell David the difficult truth? Emily's mother always said that the truth will always come out, no matter how hard a person works to conceal it—and a lie would always come back to slap you in the face.

Now Emily had to let the one lie she had ever held onto fly free—and probably slap her in the face.

She found a quiet bench behind the massive Hestia, a dim corner where surely no one could see her in her dark red walking gown and veiled bonnet. Only now, as she prepared herself to be completely and totally honest, did she realize that, in only the few days since she met David again, she had come to depend on his smiles. They had the power to make all else vanish—Georgina's worry over Emily's lack of betrothal, all her unsatisfactory suitors, her mother's chair-bound state in her dower house, her own restlessness at life in London. None of it mattered one jot when she was with David, just driving in the park or eating an ice or dancing. In that shop, laughing together at his daughter's antics and choosing gifts to send to his family, she had forgotten everything but the three of them in a golden circle—she, David, and little Anjali. Even the jewel tucked into her reticule disappeared.

With David, she was no longer restless. No longer bored or angry. She felt only—peace. A sense of some belonging.

She owed him so much, for *that* if for nothing else. She could never repay him for all that his friendship meant to her. But she could at least give him the truth.

Even if that meant he would never speak to her again, and she lost both him and his delightful daughter.

Emily stared up at Hestia, as if she could read some encouragement, some acknowledgment of the rightness of what she did, in the hard curves of marble drapery. But there was nothing. Only cold, still beauty.

She closed her eyes and imagined what it must be like to be imprisoned inside that chilly stone, to struggle to burst forth into the warmth of the sun and be free . . .

Her wild fancies were ended by the sound of footfalls—booted footfalls that ended right next to her secluded bench. Her eyes flew open, and she stared up into David's face.

His expression was veiled by the shadow falling from Hestia; the curves of his dark blue greatcoat almost made him appear to be cloaked in marble drapery himself. A beam of dusty light touched his hair and brow, and a smile whispered over his beautiful lips.

"Is this seat occupied, my lady?" he said, a teasing note lurking in his voice.

Emily laughed, and teased back, "I *was* enjoying my solitary reverie, but I might be persuaded to give it up for *you*, sirrah, if you care to bide with me for a moment."

"I can 'bide with you' happily all afternoon," he said, dropping down to sit beside her. The bench was small and narrow, forcing them into close proximity. Their sleeves brushed, silk catching on wool, and Emily was very aware of his sandalwood scent, the shadowed dark skin of his jaw. "I am quite exhausted after fending off Anjali's entreaties to come along this afternoon. She was more excited than I have ever seen her after our shopping expedition!"

"She is a lovely child," Emily said warmly. She would never have imagined she would say that after their strained hour at Gunter's, but the morning of wrapping saris and being drawn around the shop by Anjali's small hand erased that utterly.

"She is an unruly monkey," David answered, but the proud gleam in his eyes gave the lie to those stern words. "I thought the poor shopgirl would have an apoplexy when Anjali began unrolling that bolt. But Anjali *is* very pretty, I grant you—entirely due to her mother, I am sure. I sometimes think she is a magical elf-child, left in my house by mistake."

Anjali's mother. David's wife. Of course. They had fallen so easily into their old friendship that Emily sometimes forgot that years had separated them. Years which, for David, involved marriage and a new family.

"Were you married very long?" she asked quietly.

David glanced down at where their arms touched, his smile fading away into solemnity. "Almost five years. We were married when we were very young—I was eighteen, Rupasri only fifteen, though that was considered old in her family. She was the granddaughter of a friend of my grandmother; they hoped that stronger ties between the old Bengali families would give us a greater united front against the English."

"So, you did not—love her?" Emily knew she should not ask such things. They were none of her business, and, really, she was not so very sure she wanted to know the answers. But it was already out there, escaped from her own mouth into the cool air of the museum.

And she needed to know.

David glanced at her, his dark gaze opaque. She could read no answers in that at all. "Love her? I never met her before we were married. But I did come to care for her. She had a gentleness and a sweetness about her. I see those same qualities in Anjali, but I also hope that she will grow up with an independence and self-will her mother could never have hoped for. That is the only way she will be strong enough to make her way in this difficult world."

"Does Anjali miss her mother a great deal?" Emily asked gently. She remembered how she had felt when her father died—so scared and confused, so very alone. Her heart ached for the poor child—even if it twinged with jealousy for her "gentle and sweet" mother.

Those were two words no one had ever used to describe Emily.

"I am not sure if she does any longer. Rupasri died when Anjali was very young, still in leading strings. I try to tell her stories about her mother, so that she will not forget. Stories about our life in India."

"What *was* your life like in India, David? I have wondered so often since we parted. I read many books about the land, talked to people who had been there, but it still seems strange to me. Like another world."

"Yes." David turned his head to give her an intent glance, his expression unreadable. "You did tell me you read about India."

"Your stories when we were children always intrigued me. I could never imagine then that there *could* be a world outside Fair Oak, let alone one so full of heat and light and noise."

He nodded, and his gaze turned away from her toward one of the long friezes on the wall. "There is certainly plenty of all three of those in India. And scents! When we first landed in England, Anjali said the air smelled of—nothing. That was before we came into London proper, of course, but there were no spices, no perfumes, no smoke. And our townhouse is not very much like our house in Calcutta, though I tried to make Anjali's rooms as similar as I could."

Emily braced her chin on her hand, watching him with fascination. He seemed a million miles away from her at that moment, his dark eyes seeing something beyond the Marbles, beyond even herself. "Tell me about your house there," she urged.

His voice was quiet and deep as he spoke of that home, pale stucco drowsing behind a garden heavy with red and orange and white flowers, lotus and marigolds and jasmine, rich greenery heavy with the humidity hanging over all. Anjali collected pets there—a gazelle and a squirrel, as well as two little dogs the governor-general's wife gave her—and they gamboled about under the draping pipal trees. In the mornings, servants hurried along the galleries, bearing trays of sweetmeats and tea, hanging out laundry, chasing the pets away from blossoms left on homemade shrines in the garden.

In the hot afternoons, when the light bore down like a bright white-yellow pall and spirits turned heavy, everything slowed down. Carved wooden shutters were closed, canvas shelters lowered over the galleries. Anjali would drowse there with her dogs, lying against the silk cushions while her ayah sang soft songs to her. David would sit close to her with his portable desk and his work, shooing the flying insects away from his documents with the quills of his pens.

In the evenings, the shutters opened again, letting night breezes and starlight sweep through the long, low rooms. Music would drift up over the walls, chanting and the rich strains of sitars. Even when he went out to a party at the home of one of the Anglo gentry, that music would trail after him, sweet and seductive.

Emily closed her eyes as he spoke, seeing all of this

in her mind. The flowers, the heavy air, the music, even
the pet gazelle—it all came to vivid, colorful life for her.
Only very gradually did she realize that David had
ceased speaking, his voice trailing away into the cool
marble around them.

She opened her eyes, half-surprised to find herself not
in an Indian gallery but in the dim environs of the British
Museum. And to find David watching her.

She summoned up a small, strained smile for him. "It
sounds—amazing. I imagine I will never see it, though."

"And why is that?"

"A lady—a duke's sister—could never hope to travel
so very far alone. Alex and my mother might allow me
to go to Brighton or maybe even France or Italy, but
hardly Calcutta! Your words took me there, though. It
must be just as I imagine it—strange and unearthly
beautiful. How glorious your life must have been there!
I always thought it must be."

"I thought of you over all those years, too, Emily.
Every day, I think." He leaned closer to her, their arms
and shoulders pressed together, warm and intimate even
through layers of silk and wool and blasted propriety. "I
wondered what your life was like, how you were growing up. What you would be like as a lady."

Emily stared at him, mesmerized. She had always
thought about him, of course, but she had imagined he
forgot about her in that new life of his. She was just the
silly, tomboyish girl who followed him all about, and in
Calcutta he was surely surrounded by kohl-eyed beauties.

The thought that he had remembered her, speculated
on her growing-up, was intoxicating.

"And how did I grow up?" she whispered.

He grinned at her, his dimples flashing enticingly.
"Extraordinarily well, I would say. You are beautiful,
Emily. And so kind to everyone, especially my daughter.

You have not been hardened by London Society, as so many are. The years have been good to you."

At this reminder of the past, of what she had truly come here to tell him, Emily turned away from the glow in his eyes. She stared at Hestia's draperies, suddenly deeply chilled. She wrapped her arms about herself, and murmured, "They were not always so fine as they are now—the years, I mean."

"What are you talking about, Emily? Your family is obviously happy, and no lady of the *ton* could have a lovelier smile than you do."

"I lost my smile for a long time. Before Alex came back from Spain and met Georgina, many things happened to my family. Things I would want to never think of again."

"Then do not think of them!" David seized her hand in his, his gloved fingers strong around her own. "Emily, the last thing I would want to do is make you unhappy, make you speak of unpleasant matters you would rather forget. I would be a poor friend to bring even a speck of unhappiness into your life."

Emily folded her free hand around their clasped fingers, holding them together. She stared hard at their embrace, unable to look into his eyes, his beautiful face. If she even glimpsed him, she could never tell him this.

"No, David, I must say these things to you. I must tell you the truth; it is why I met you here today. But please, please don't utter a word until I am finished."

"Very well, Emily," he answered softly. "Tell me anything you like. I will listen."

Still clinging to his hand, Emily took a deep breath and launched into her old tale. She told him all about her mother's riding accident soon after David and his father left England—the accident that left her still confined to her chair. She spoke of her father's death, and Damien's disastrous reign as duke. Of how their sudden lack of fortune left her to make ends meet at Fair Oak, to take care of their mother and maintain their good name.

Finally, she came to the day Damien took the Star away. She squeezed her eyes shut as tightly as she could and sped through the story, her voice cracking.

". . . and so you see, David," she finished. "I know that you wanted to ask me about the Star; I am sure you must want it back. It is yours! And my family stole it. I am so very sorry. I can never say that enough. You must hate me now. You must be sorry you ever stood as my friend!"

David said nothing, but neither did he let go of her hand. His clasp tightened around hers convulsively, and she felt the stiffness of his shoulder against hers.

Slowly, very slowly, she opened her eyes and dared to peek up at him. He stared away, over her head, and his handsome features were taut. He was the very portrait of suppressed anger.

Emily tried to pull her hand from his, to move her loathsome presence away so he would not have to look at her and her betrayal. But he refused to release her. Indeed, his other arm came around her shoulders and held her close. His eyes as he stared down at her were burning black.

"How dare he?" David growled, in a voice she had never heard from him before. "A brother is meant to protect his sister, to hold her safe, not throw her into poverty and dishonor. How could Damien have even called himself a man after such disgrace? He had no honor. No strength."

Emily felt a prickling behind her eyes, a harbinger of tears. She could *not* cry now! She had refused to show tears for all this time, refused to be less than perfectly proud. Even when neighbors whispered and snickered about her old gowns, she would not lower her chin an inch. She was a Kenton, and Kentons were *never* ashamed, even when their hearts burned with it.

She blinked hard, and said thickly, "He—he had a sickness for gambling, and for other shameful things as well."

"Drink and whores? That is no excuse, Emily. He was a duke. He owed his family and title a great responsibility. And he did not fulfill it. He left his mother behind to illness, his sister to hard work a lady should never know—and he ended by stealing from my family."

"I should have stopped him!" Emily cried, frantic. "I should have known he would come for the Star and hidden it from him. I should have run after him when he took it—"

"Emily!" David said firmly, seizing her by the shoulders and forcing her to face him, to be still. "None of this is on your head. None of it! You were always honorable. You took care of your mother and your tenants when your brothers could not. You never could have saved the Star from Damien's greed—no one could."

Emily did cry then. Great, salty tears that ran down her cheeks and splashed onto David's wrist. She pressed hard at her lips with her gloved hand, but the tears would not be stopped. She had thought David would hate her when he discovered what happened. Instead, he was angry with *Damien*. He called her honorable, he held her close to him.

For so long, she had felt all alone, even in Alex and Georgina's warm home. Now, suddenly, she was *not* alone. It was too much for all her locked-up emotions to bear.

"I should have tried harder to stop him," she sniffled. "You were my best friend, David, and I disappointed you."

He gave her a wry smile. "Emily, you could never, ever disappoint me." He reached inside his coat for a handkerchief and pressed it into her hand. "Now, here, my brave girl. Dry your eyes before someone notices us and we are ejected from the museum for causing a scene."

Emily gave a watery laugh, and mopped at her eyes and cheeks. Now that a measure of her good sense was returning, she was glad their corner was so ill-lit—her face was surely a mottled mess. "Indeed, you are right. Damien was the one who took the Star, but I am the one left with the consequences. I know you wanted it back, David."

He sat back on the bench, stretching his long legs out before him with a deep sigh. "Yes, I did. Or rather, my grandmother did. Does."

"Your grandmother?"

"Ah, yes. You see, Emily, I have my own tale to tell you."

"A tale?" Emily said warily. "I like tales—usually. Unless they are like my own."

David smiled gently. "You say you enjoy stories of India. And this one is full of curses and spirits and all manner of exciting events. And, according to my grandmother, it is even true."

Emily was intrigued, despite everything there was to worry about at this moment. There was a childlike part of herself, hidden in her heart, that did still revel in fairy tales. "About the Star?"

"Yes. You see, when my grandparents were first married, they were unable to have a child. My grandmother made many sacrifices, visited many shrines. One night, after praying at a temple to the god Shiva, she had a vision."

"A vision?"

"A dream, if you will. She dreamed that Shiva, who is a god of contradictions—the dance and stillness, bounty and wrath, destruction and fertility—told her he would grant her wish if she would bring him the great sky-stone. The most beautiful of all jewels."

Emily was mesmerized by the flow of his deep, rich voice, and the strange story he told. In her mind's eye, she could see his grandmother as a beautiful, dark young woman swathed in bright silks, kneeling at the feet of the many-armed god. "And that was the Star?"

"The Star of India, yes. It belonged to my great-grandfather. He wore it in his turban, and was deeply proud of it. In a land of glorious jewels, the Star was special. But, as much as he treasured the jewel, he treasured the dream of grandsons even more."

"So, he gave her the sapphire."

"He did. And, that very same day, she and my grandfather went back to the temple and laid the Star at Shiva's feet. Nine months later, my uncle was born. Six more children followed, including my mother, who was said the be the most beautiful woman in Bengal."

"The sacrifice worked!"

"It would appear so."

"But then what went wrong?"

"My mother grew up, and met my father, who was in the army in Calcutta. They met in the marketplace and fell instantly in love. She wanted to give him something extraordinary to prove the depth of her devotion. The finest thing she knew of was the Star. She saw it often, for my grandmother liked to take her children back to the temple to make sacrifices in thanks."

"Was your mother not afraid to take the jewel from its sacred spot?" Emily whispered.

A ghost of a smile drifted across David's lips. "My mother was not a superstitious woman. She converted to Christianity when she married my father, and she did not fear Shiva's wrath. Very soon after she gave him the Star, and when I was a small child, my father's older brother died and he was called back to England to take up the earldom. Only after my parents departed Calcutta did my grandmother discover what her daughter had done."

"And then what did she do?" Emily asked.

"I was only a tiny child then, but my grandmother's servants say she wailed and cried, and broke everything in her chambers. She went back to the temple to beg forgiveness, and that night she had another dream."

"Or vision."

"Yes, another vision. Shiva said that her family would be cursed until the Star was returned to him."

"Oh," Emily breathed. In her imagination, the museum around them had disappeared completely. She was in a humid-heavy temple, surrounded by the thick scents of incense and jasmine—feeling the inescapable weight of a curse falling over herself and her family. She could not breathe; her breath caught in her throat, strangling her.

Emily reached up to loosen the ribbons of her bonnet, trying not to reveal the depth of her reaction. She hated for David to think her an even bigger fool than he surely already did. "What happened?"

David shrugged. "It appeared her curse came true. My mother died very young, in childbirth. My father nearly went mad with grief, and he died of yellow fever soon after we returned to India. Rupasri also died young."

Emily's family, too, had been touched by this litany of despair, she realized with a shock. Her mother's accident, her father's early death, Damien's wasted life. Could it all have been the fault of the Star?

Do not be stupid, Emily, she told herself sternly. *This is the nineteenth century, not the Middle Ages. There are no such things as curses.*

Still, a tiny sense of disquiet reverberated in her heart.

"Do—do you believe in this curse, David?" she said slowly.

He stared at her closely. "No. Bad things happen to all

of us in this world. I suppose it *is* a curse, but the curse is called life."

"Yes. Of course."

"However, my grandmother believes entirely in this curse. Before I left India, she charged me with recovering the jewel. I love her, Emily—she was like a true mother to me when my parents died. She is very old now, and I do not want her to live out the rest of her years uneasy because of this."

Emily's heart ached for him. "I am so sorry, David. What a dreadful thing!"

"Are you sure you have no idea where the Star could be now? Where your brother sold it?"

"I . . ." Emily swallowed hard. Her stare dropped to her lap, to the braid trim on her gown. She had been so lost in the tale of the Star in India that she quite forgot her own story was not finished. The hardest part was still to come. "Do you read the London papers, David?"

He gave a rueful laugh. "I do try, but I fear I cannot read too closely when Anjali is at the breakfast table with me."

"But you do remember Sir Charles and Lady Innis? We met them in the park."

One of his dark brows arched quizzically. "Yes, I remember them. I received an invitation to some ball they are giving. What does all of this have to do with the Star?"

"Well, you see, Sir Charles has the Star—or at least the false Star Damien sold him. It is the paste copy which will be on display at this ball, which the experts will then examine. But I have no idea where the real one can be. I have wracked my brain trying to recall every pawnshop Damien frequented, every gaming hell he owed money to, but it is no use! I am sorry, David—so very sorry."

"Emily, I have told you, none of this is your fault.

How could it possibly be? I shall just have to—" Suddenly, David's soothing words broke off. His dark stare veered back to her sharply, and he reached out to clasp her arm. "Did you say experts were coming to examine the paste Star?"

Emily nodded mutely. Her voice seemed to have died in her throat, and she was weary—so very weary. The high tension of the past few days had ground her down, and her very bones were tired. She longed to rest her head against David's strong shoulder and sleep for a month. She wanted to forget all about her family and the jewel, and everything except David.

But that could not be. She had come this far, she could not stop now, not with everything yet undone and the sword of Damocles still hanging over her head. The best she could hope for was that David would help her, be her ally.

She stared deeply into his eyes, but all she saw there were more difficult questions.

"Yes," she answered. "And they will know at once that the stone is false—and Sir Charles will remember that it was my brother who sold it to him all those years ago. But I have a plan, you see. Or at least the beginnings of one. That is why I was at that jeweler's shop in Gracechurch Street this morning."

Still watching him closely, Emily told of her wild idea to switch out the new Star with the paste one at the ball. How she would contrive to do this, she was not entirely certain. She could only hope there would be a moment when no one else was near the case holding the Star. Then she could employ the old lock-picking skills she had perfected as a girl, when breaking into cases was the only way she could obtain needed coins from Damien. The switch could be done in a trice. If only . . .

Her plan was only half-done, she knew that. And that

conclusion was confirmed by the dubious expression on David's face.

"It is ridiculous, is it not?" she said, pulling away from him.

"Not entirely, Emily. The idea of replacing the paste jewel with a genuine sapphire is a very clever one. But you must not get caught in making the switch. You need a better plan for that part of it." He stared past her, at the impervious Hestia. Slowly, resolutely, dubiousness turned to calculation. A smile broke over his face, as the golden sunrise after a very dark night. "You will need assistance. From someone like myself, perhaps."

Emily's heart lightened, as if on new-sprung wings, and she could not stop herself from leaning forward to press a kiss to his cheek. "Oh, David! I was so, so hoping you would say that."

What a fool I am, David thought, as he left Emily with promises to think on her plans and conceive an idea for the night of the Innis ball. What was he doing, contemplating turning jewel thief (well, jewel *switcher,* which was in a way even worse)? He was an earl now, with responsibilities, a daughter to take care of. He was not a wild youth anymore, free to spend all his time running across the country fields with Emily Kenton.

He was a besotted fool. That was the only answer. One look into the sapphire depths of Emily's eyes, and he would do anything to make her smile again. Even turn burglar.

But there was no denying the way his heart seemed to skip a beat when she *did* smile. The way his blood surged and heated when her soft lips touched his skin, even briefly. He wanted to help her, to make her life perfect—now and always.

And there was also no denying the excitement that simmered in his soul at the prospect of intrigue. Life in

England was quiet and staid in comparison with the hot, bright drama of India. Only with Emily did he feel himself come truly alive again, did he hear the distant call of wild birds tempting him onward.

He swung up into his phaeton, turning the horses toward home. Emily's carriage, a proper one this time, with the Kenton crest on the door, had already moved onto the next street, out of his sight.

The thought of the shameful way her brother had treated her made his blood burn hot in his veins. His heart cried out for revenge—yet that could never be. Damien Kenton was dead, forever beyond an earthly reckoning for his dishonorable deeds. He had been dead for many years, and still Emily was cleaning up his messes. Beautiful, sweet Emily, whose young days should have been filled with music and gowns and suitors, not money and farms and family honor.

What was wrong with Alexander and his vivid, clever wife, that they could not see the unbearable pressure their sister was living under?

But that was unfair. Emily had not gone to them for help, insisted they not be "bothered" in anyway by this debacle. He, David, was all she had. He could not disappoint her.

The loss of the Star was a great one, and he felt it keenly. His grandmother had charged him with its recovery, and he never wanted to disappoint her, either. He would give his left arm to release her from her "curse" and ease her old age.

Yet, even more strongly, with a force greater than any he had ever encountered before, he wanted to see Emily laugh again—really laugh, as she had when they were children. Free of all worry and care. He would do anything for that. He would die for it.

Oh-ray-baba. He was a besotted fool, indeed.

Chapter Ten

"*W*ell, well," Georgina murmured, sotto voce, as they left their wraps with the waiting footmen and melded into the throng flowing into the Innis ballroom. "It would seem that even the highest sticklers of the *ton* have allowed curiosity to get the better of them. They have all deigned to enter the house of a 'vulgar Cit.'"

Emily adjusted her kid gloves over her arms and gave her sister-in-law a wry smile. She was trying her hardest to appear cool and amused, as she usually was at such events. She even laughed a bit, but she could see that she had not entirely fooled Georgina, who watched Emily with a tiny frown puckering her forehead.

Before Georgina could say anything, Emily turned away to snatch a glass of champagne from the tray of a passing footman. As she sipped, or rather gulped in a most unladylike fashion at the bracing, bubbling liquid, her gaze scanned the crowd.

It was just as Georgina said—everyone who was anyone in Society was there, despite the fact that many of them declared their intentions of never setting foot in such a "mushroom's" dwelling. Obviously, the burning desire to see the interior arrangements of one of London's largest houses had overcome even snobbery. Emily couldn't help but be a bit glad, despite the anxiety that made her heart pound and her hands tremble. She rather liked Sir Charles and his stylish wife, and if not for the unfortunate circumstance of the Star she would have enjoyed knowing them better. Perhaps in the future—far in the future. . . .

Lady Innis, clad in a very fashionable and stunning gown of a cloth-of-gold tunic over an ivory satin slip, was in radiant form. She greeted and laughed, and gestured with her gold-colored feather fan, trailed by her bemused husband. Lady Innis's diamond necklace and earrings, as well as the large ruby brooch that fastened her gold silk turban, were the grandest Emily had ever seen.

No wonder they can afford to donate the Star, she thought. They obviously wanted the philanthropic prestige of patronizing a new, highbrow museum more than they needed money.

She exchanged her empty glass for a full one and drifted along the edges of the white and silver ballroom, trying to stay out of sight of any of her friends or acquaintances. She saw Mr. Carrington over by the tall windows, but he did not spot her.

The dancing had not yet started, but the orchestra, hidden behind a bank of potted palms, played a soft melody. Mozart, perhaps, or Haydn. Emily could hear it well, because, despite the great size of the gathering, the crowd was strangely hushed. People stood in clusters and knots, whispering and murmuring and staring. She found a quiet corner, half-hidden behind a palm of her own, and scanned the faces carefully.

But the one face she wanted to see above all others was not to be glimpsed. David had obviously not yet arrived.

"Please, do not let him forget," she whispered, half in prayer, half to reassure herself. He would not forget, how

could he? Her tale had been one of the oddest he had
surely ever heard, and the Star was almost as much his
concern as it was hers. But maybe he had decided she
was an utter lunatic and he wanted no part in her
schemes.

Perhaps he was on his way back to Calcutta even
now! And, really, Emily could not blame him if he was.
But she needed him. Not just on this evening, but on
every evening to come.

The champagne glass almost slipped out of her hand
at this revelation, which had come out of the darkness
not as a lightning bolt, but as a whisper of music on
flower-scented air. The thought of David going back to
India did not give her such a sharp pang because she
needed his help with the Star—but because she loved
him. Not as a child loved her friend, but as a woman
loved a man.

Emily took another deep gulp of her champagne, and
it helped to clear the sudden misty haze at the edges of
her vision. Yes—she did! She *loved* David. In truth, she
had never ceased to love him, not over all the years they
were parted. But since he had first come back, since she
had first seen him at the Wilton ball, her feelings had
been so very different. The dark, mysterious depths of
his eyes, his elegant hands, so strong when they held
hers. The way he laughed at her foibles, the echo of his
voice as he told her of the exotic mysteries of India . . .

She wanted to clasp all those things to her and never,
ever let them go. When she was with him, she never felt
that aching restlessness that had plagued her of late.
With him, she was always at peace, even in the midst of
all this turmoil over the wretched Star. When he sat beside her and held her hand in his, she knew nothing
could go wrong.

When she was alone, as now, her stomach tied itself

into knots, and she was certain her schemes could only go horribly awry.

He surely did not feel the same about her. He had been married, had known the serenity of a beautiful Indian wife—a wife lovely enough to produce the doll-child Anjali. Emily was not a serene woman. She never had been. And the Star was still lost to David's family, no matter what happened here tonight. Her own family had caused that, and even David's understanding could not erase it.

After all this trouble was over, David might try to distance himself and his daughter from her—or he would if he was sensible. But maybe, just maybe, once they were all settled in the country, away from London, she could show him that there was more to her than trouble and wild schemes. She could show him how much she knew about farming, could perhaps advise him on his fields or teach Anjali how to ride.

"One plan at a time, Emily," she whispered.

Oh, horrors! Now she was talking to herself. This would all have to end soon, or she would surely have to be sent to Bedlam.

And her champagne was all gone. She turned her head to see if perhaps there was any more to be had, any tray-laden footmen nearby. As she peered around fruitlessly in search of refreshment, a low, hissing murmur floated through the potted palm to her ears.

"Look, there is the Indian earl!" a voice, which Emily recognized as that of the draconian Lady Linley, said. "How very dark he is. I see nothing at all of his father in him. How handsome that man was in his youth! We could scarce believe he made such a *mésalliance*."

"Perhaps the new earl's father was really the punkah boy!" her companion said, with a nasty little snicker. "One does hear such things about native women . . ."

How dare they! Those shrill old harridans. Emily's

face flamed, and her mouth turned dry and sour. If only she truly was the Boudicca David named her. She would run them over with her chariot. Skewer them with her sword.

But she was not Boudicca. She was simply Lady Emily Kenton. And that title might stand her in better stead here in this ballroom than a spear would. There was only one thing she could do.

She deposited her empty glass at the base of the palm, made certain her hair and gown were tidy, and marched out with her head held high. She swept past the two witches without even glancing at them, her gaze searching the crowd for David. Her Indian earl.

He was speaking with their hostess, too far away to have heard the old gossips' comments—but surely he had heard it before, and worse. It was just such cuts, small but bleeding, that had driven his father back to India.

But they would *not* drive David away. Not if Emily had anything to say about it.

My brother is not a duke for nothing, she thought resolutely. It was high time she used that title to its full advantage.

She marched up to David, laid her hand lightly on his arm, and said, loudly enough for everyone nearby to hear, "Lord Darlinghurst! Such a pleasure to meet with you again. My brother and sister-in-law were just asking about you."

David stared down at her, his gaze startled for an instant. Then he smiled, a slow, secret smile just for her. He crooked his arm so that her hand slid securely into its warm safety, and said, "Lady Emily. How good of your brother to ask after me. I trust that your family is all well this evening?"

"Very well, thank you." Emily turned to nod at Lady Innis, who watched them with great interest. "Our families are very old friends, you see, Lady Innis. Our estates march together."

"Indeed, Lady Emily?" Lady Innis said brightly. "Fascinating!"

"And I must compliment you on your lovely arrangements, also, Lady Innis," Emily went on. "The colors are stunning."

"Oh, thank you!" Lady Innis said, her voice even brighter. "I was not at all sure about the silver . . ."

"It is very stylish." Emily glanced about, but she did not see Sir Charles. Nor did she see the object of her pursuit—the Star. "Is your grand jewel not to be displayed this evening, Lady Innis? I have been so eager to catch a glimpse of it again. I have not seen it since I was a tiny child."

Lady Innis gave a little trill of laughter. "Of course, Lady Emily! My husband is so immensely proud of his treasure, I doubt you could escape a glimpse even if you wished it. He has gone now to be sure all is in readiness. It will be displayed in the library. I will make certain you are among the first to see it. But now, you must excuse me—I have to instruct the musicians to begin playing for the dancing."

"Of course, Lady Innis. Thank you so much." Emily watched their hostess hurry away, feeling David watching *her* all the while.

The crowd surged around them toward the dance floor, but the two of them stayed exactly where they were, arms linked, as if suddenly turned into the Grecian statues they viewed only the day before.

"You look beautiful, Lady Emily," David said quietly. His cool breath stirred the curls at her temple, and she shivered despite the cloying warmth of the ballroom. "You could almost be a sapphire yourself."

Emily laughed. She had not chosen her gown, an iridescent deep blue silk with silver embroidery on the

small bodice and puffed sleeves, apurpose to imitate the
Star, but it appeared as if she had. She reached up to
straighten the band of blue silk holding back her hair,
and said, "At least I did not wear my sapphire combs!
That would have been too much indeed."

"But I see you did wear *this*." David, his gaze suddenly intent, reached out to touch the ring that hung on
its chain near the lace edge of her neckline. She had
worn it out tonight, for all to see, after all the years of
keeping it hidden.

"Yes," she answered softly. "I always wear this
ring—next to my heart. Do you remember when you
gave it to me?"

"Of course. I remember it very well." The corner of
his lips quirked. "It does not appear to have protected
you very well."

"Oh, but it has! I always thought that since you gave
it to me . . ." But she could not go on. The press of people was too heavy around them, and such things were not
meant to be discussed in crowded ballrooms. They were
meant for gardens under moonlight, silent and scented
with flowers—and dark, so her blushes could not be
seen.

He seemed to know what she was thinking, feeling.
He gave a short nod, and said, "Would you care to dance
with me, Lady Emily?"

"Yes, thank you, Lord Darlinghurst. That would be
most—pleasant."

As they moved to take their places in the set, David
whispered, "And then perhaps we can catch a glimpse of
this little stone that has caused so many difficulties."

The Innises' library was almost as vast as their ballroom, but it was dark and cavernous rather than all airy
silver light. Shelves full of books, their rich leather bind-
ings uncracked as if they had never been touched, soared

to the gilded ceiling. Heavy furniture, upholstered in forest green velvet and dark red brocade, lurked in the shadows, crouched like jungle creatures ready to pounce on Emily if she made a suspicious move.

The only light in the room came from two tall candelabra fitted with white wax tapers. They were situated on either side of a glass case, casting a sparkling glow on its crystalline edges. A narrow Aubuosson runner in pale shades of blue and cream led to the case.

Emily knew that her feet must be moving along that carpet, because the case was drawing ever closer, but she was not the one controlling them. Now that her goal was literally within her sight, she felt numb, surrounded by a cold mist. Even her lips were chilled.

Only her hand on David's arm held her upright.

"It feels as if we are about to be presented the Holy Grail," she whispered to him, her gaze never leaving the back of Sir Charles's green velvet coat as he led them further and further into the library.

David laughed softly, but his head did not incline to look down at her. When she glanced up at him, she saw that he was taking in the entire room, his dark eyes darting from crevice to corner.

"What are you looking at?" she said, again in a hoarse whisper.

"Sh," he answered. "Later."

Sir Charles halted next to the glistening case, his florid face rapt as he stared into it. "And this, Lady Emily and Lord Darlinghurst, is my treasure. The finest piece in my collection. I am so happy to be able to show it to you tonight." His glance moved from the case to Emily, his brows suddenly raised in seeming astonished remembrance. "Oh, but you must have seen it before, Lady Emily! For indeed it was your late brother who sold it to me, years ago. An act for which I will always be grateful."

Emily forced her frozen lips to stretch into a smile. She hoped it *looked* less like a rictus than it *felt*. "Of course, Sir Charles. But I am sure your great appreciation for the jewel far exceeds any he ever possessed."

"Oh, I *have* appreciated it, I do assure you, Lady Emily! But now I must not be selfish with it any longer. Everyone should be able to see such wondrous beauty, which is why I am donating it to the Mercer Museum."

Emily swallowed hard past her dry throat. "That is very commendable of you, Sir Charles."

"Oh, well—but you must take a proper look! Come closer, Lady Emily. And you, too, Lord Darlinghurst. I know you have spent many years in India, so you will be able to appreciate the fine workmanship."

Emily dropped her hand from David's arm and took a tiny step toward the case, then another, until she was so close that her breath left a small cloud on the glass.

The paste Star looked magnificent, lying there on a bed of luminous white satin. Whoever Damien had hired to make the copy had done an excellent job. If she did not know the truth, she would not have been able to see it. The paste sapphire gleamed a deep sea blue, set off by the ring of false diamonds. It was beautiful, truly, yet it lacked—something. Some ineffable draw that only the true Star, wherever it was, could possess.

Her gaze dropped from the stone to the case itself, to the tiny locked hinge. A thin wire, carefully bent, would take care of it easily enough, if she had space and time to concentrate.

That time was not tonight. Sir Charles watched her avidly, waiting for her to say something.

"It is beautiful, Sir Charles," she murmured. "Obviously, it has prospered under your care."

Sir Charles beamed. "Thank you, Lady Emily! I have loved it very much. My wife has sometimes wished to wear it, but I have insisted that it stay here, safely locked away. The risk of theft is always great if one is known to have such an object."

"You are very wise." Emily stepped back from the case. She could not stand the glaring light any longer, and her fingers itched to snatch open the case right then and there and be done with it.

Patience, she told herself. *You knew this would not be quick or simple.*

Patience, though, had never been Emily's strong point.

"I know that most of your guests are eager for a glimpse of the Star," Emily said. "So, we will not monopolize your time any further, Sir Charles. It was most kind of you to give us the first peek."

"Indeed, Sir Charles," David added. "It is a very fine piece."

"Thank you, thank you," Sir Charles muttered, his attention still focused on his treasure.

David clasped Emily's arm and led her out of the library into the deserted corridor. If possible, it was even darker than the library—a long expanse of blackness broken only by brief intervals where the wall sconces cast out tiny splashes of tawny light. There was one large square of moonlight, spreading from a half-open glass door that led out to a narrow terrace and tiny garden.

David drew her out of the door onto that terrace, where they leaned against the cold marble balustrade.

Emily was grateful for its chill solidity holding her up. She had not realized how tense her muscles had been, how tired she was, until this moment. Oh, why could this whole matter not be over and done with? She was sick of the Star, sick of the whole deceitful thing. She wished she was far from here, riding her horse at Fair Oak, the sun on her face and the smell of green hay in her nostrils.

Then David put his arms around her, drawing her

away from the cold stone, and she thought, *Well, perhaps here is not such a bad place after all.*

In fact, as she laid her hand against his chest and felt the steady thrum of his heartbeat, she knew there was no place in the world she would rather be. She had always hated Damien for the untenable position he had put her in. Now, she was almost grateful. If it was not for what he had done with the Star, she would not be here on this terrace, with David's arms around her.

She inhaled his clean scent of starched linen and sandalwood soap, and thought whimsically, *Thank you, Damien.* She twined her arms around David and drew him even closer.

She felt him rest his cheek against her hair. In this moment, she could forget all about her dilemma, her family—everything but the beauty of this instant, the sweet peace in her heart.

Peace was one thing she had not known in a very long time, and it was like laudanum to her restless heart—she craved it, *needed* it. Just as she needed laughter and contentment and new thoughts and sights.

All of those things David, and David alone, brought to her. Why could this moment not go on and on forever?

She felt David's shoulder shift against her, and she tilted back her head to stare up at him. His face was all sharp planes and angles in the moonlight, the silver glow playing over his high cheekbones and the sensual fullness of his lips.

He was like a god himself, she reflected dreamily. An exotic god of the night and the moon. He needed only to be rid of his fashionably cut coat and brocade waistcoat, though, and draped in pearls and ropes of rubies. A silken turban should be wound about his head, fastened with the Star itself . . .

This reminder of the Star brought her back to earth with a prosaic thud. *That* was truly why they were here, brought to the Innis house by her own crazy schemes. As much as she wanted to lose herself in romantic fantasy, she could not. Not yet. Maybe not ever.

"I am sorry, David," she whispered.

He gave her a lazy smile, one finger catching at her curls and twining them like skeins of silk over his skin. "For what, Boudicca?"

"For bringing you into this hopeless business. You should be at home with Anjali, planning your new life at Combe Lodge, not darting around London with me, trying to figure out how to break and enter . . ."

"Emily, no," he said, shaking his head at her. "For almost the past year, I was on a ship, perishing of boredom and trying to find ways to amuse Anjali so she would not feel the same. I thought that once we were in England the boredom would vanish and I would be far too busy to ever think of it again. But it was not true."

"Was it not?"

"No. You see, I had forgotten how very gray England can be. Gray sky, gray buildings, even gray people. I felt more restless than ever. I did not see color again until you appeared before me at that ball." He leaned down and kissed her brow, the tip of her nose. Tiny, feather-light kisses that warmed her to her very toes.

She leaned into him, trying to grasp that warmth and forget her misgivings about their mission.

But it would not be entirely dismissed. It kept clamoring in her mind, not letting her revel in her new feelings. "But we still have not switched the two Stars . . ."

"Sh!" He caught her face between his hands, holding her still so she must look up at him. His thumbs gently brushed the curls back from her temples. "We will. Just not tonight. I have the beginnings of a plan."

His caress was drugging, turning her blood to a warm rush, lulling her into a glorious haze. "A—plan?" she murmured, going up on tiptoe to kiss his jaw, the skin

like satin beneath her lips. She could not help herself—
something *made* her do it, some imp of mischief in her
mind. "What sort of a plan?"

"I will tell you all about it—later." His strong touch
moved down her throat to her shoulders, holding her
away from him by just a fraction of an inch. A small,
cool breeze flowed between them. "If you will tell me
why you wear my ring." His thumb hooked into the
chain, lifting the ring up to her view. The edge of his nail
rasped against her bare flesh, making her shiver.

Emily stared at her ring, sparkling in the starlight. The
true, simple answer was that she wore the ring because
she loved him. Without knowing it, she had been waiting
for him all these years. That was why she had never accepted any of her suitors.

But she could not tell him that. It would make her
sound too silly, like the girls in the Minerva Press novels
Georgina loved so much.

She covered his hand with hers, pulling the ring back
down, out of sight. "I wear it for protection, which you
promised it would give me."

He tilted his head, watching her closely. "And do you
think it worked?"

"Of course." She gave a little laugh. "I am as healthy
as a country horse, and I always have been. And I have a
very good life." She turned her head to stare up at the
glorious night sky, black velvet spread with glowing
jewels of stars. "Look at this night—the moon, the garden, a moment alone with you, away from that horribly
stuffy ballroom. Who could ever want more?"

Then, to stop him from pressing her to say more—
and because she just really, truly wanted to—she slid her
hands behind his neck and pulled him down to her. Her
lips met his, and all else was forgotten.

*   *   *

David had never tasted anything as sweet as Emily's lips. They were finer than honey or pistachio cream. Her breath was cool where it mingled with his in a great rush, sending purest life through his very veins. He pulled her against him, his hands sliding down the silken back of her gown, their bodies pressed together until he did not know where *he* ended and *she* began. Her rose-petal perfume filled his senses, clouding all else.

The night was cool around them, but his skin was heated as if by a Calcutta summer. He needed Emily—needed her like water, like air.

That sudden realization made him step back from her, holding her by the waist as she swayed. Such need, such *desperation*, had no place in this night, in this situation. Anyone could come along to this terrace and spy their embrace. Gossip about Lady Emily Kenton and the Indian earl would spread like a fire through the Innis ballroom and out into the entire city. While David could certainly think of far worse things than being obliged to offer for Emily, of having her for his wife, he did not want it like that.

And they did still have that dratted Star to think about.

He threw back his head, taking in a deep breath of night air. What he really wanted to do was howl at the sky. He felt Emily slide out from beneath his grasp and turn away, her own shoulders heaving with the effort to breathe.

A tiny sound broke out, and David realized with shock that she was—was *crying*.

"Emily!" he cried hoarsely, catching her by the arm to turn her back to him. One small, crystal tear tracked along her cheek. Her hands shot up to cover her face, and she tried to turn away from him again. But he refused to let her go. "Emily, what is it?"

"I—I am sorry I threw myself at you," she muttered, swiping at her cheeks with her gloved fingertips. "Oh, I

am always saying I'm sorry to you! But I truly don't
know what came over me. The anxiety about the jewels . . ."

"You mean it was not my irresistible self?" he teased.

"Oh, David," Emily moaned, covering her face again.

"Emily, *shona,*" he said, taking a handkerchief from
inside his coat and pressing it into her hand. "Please,
throw yourself at me anytime you wish. I vow I do not
mind a jot. Well, you may want to refrain while we are
in a ballroom or in the middle of the Park, but other than
that . . ."

Just as he had hoped, Emily gave a choked laugh, and
then another and another. She mopped at her face with
his handkerchief, and said, "I am still sorry. I am not
usually quite so—so improper. But with everything that
has been happening . . ."

"It is really quite all right, Emily." David took her
hand in his and raised it to his lips. The thin kid tasted
faintly of the salt of her tears, which lingered on his
mouth. "You have been so very brave, shouldering your
family's burden all alone for years. But you are not alone
any longer, Boudicca, I promise you."

Emily smiled at him, a tiny, trusting ray of light that
broke across her tearstained face like the first beam of
hope in a dark, sinful world. She stepped close to him
again, slipping her hands into his. "Oh, David. Whatever
are we going to do about Sir Charles's wretched jewel?"

David was not entirely certain, as he had only the
glimmerings of a plan, but he would not tell Emily that.
Not after having reassured her that she could rely on him
and she was no longer alone. He squeezed her hands and
said, "There is nothing we can do tonight. There will be
guests in and out of that library for the rest of the ball,
gasping and sighing over the Star."

"Indeed."

"When is the stone to be transferred to the museum?"

"Next week, I believe. I am not sure. After those dreadful experts come in to inspect it." Emily's voice was quiet in the night, drained of her usual vitality. His Boudicca had obviously grown weary from fighting her Romans.

David longed to catch her in his arms, to cradle her against him until she slept and found her much-needed rest. But he could not. He did not have that right. The most he could do was tighten his hands on hers and hold her up. "That does not leave us much time. But we will find a way, Em."

"When, David? What can I do?"

"For now, you can come back into the ballroom and dance with me again, before we are missed. You can laugh at my ever so witty jokes and have a glass of champagne, and then we will eat supper with your brother and his wife. How does that sound? Can you do that for me?"

Emily laughed, and tucked his handkerchief away in her reticule. She smoothed back her hair and fluffed out her skirts. "Oh, yes. I think I can manage to do all that."

"Excellent! Then, shall we?" David held out his arm to her and they turned to stroll back inside the house, as if they were just returning from viewing the famous jewel.

And, after they danced and chatted and ate Lady Innis's fine lobster patties, David would go home to his silent house—and devise a scheme to break into Sir Charles's mansion and switch a false stone with a real one.

He was out of his mind, of course, to contemplate such a ridiculous scheme. But somehow he had never felt saner—or happier—in his life.

Chapter Eleven

*I*t was a gray day, with only a pale, watery light escaping from cracks in the low-hanging clouds. It had not rained, but it appeared as if it might at any moment. Emily did not mind the dismal weather, though, for it kept the crowds away from the Park. There were only birds, and a few hearty souls like herself in search of beneficial exercise, to watch her pace the footpath.

She wore her warmest walking dress of yellow wool, with an umbrella in her hands that she only half-remembered the butler giving her as she left the house. But she still shivered.

Where *was* David? He sent her a note this morning asking her to meet him on this very path, yet she did not see him. Every time a brisk stroller or a running child brushed past her, she started—but it was never David.

"Perhaps I am early," she muttered. She knew that she was. She had not been able to sleep at all once they returned home from the Innis ball. All she could do was lie in bed, her wide-open eyes staring up at the embroidered underside of the bed curtains, remembering the events of the night. *All* the events. But especially that kiss.

Oh, what had ever possessed her to grasp at David like that, pulling him to her like a Covent Garden doxy! She had never behaved so before; had never even been

tempted. Perhaps it was the moonlight, or the champagne. Or maybe the power of the Star was so great that
even a paste copy exuded some of its allure.

Or maybe, if she could only bring herself to admit it,
she would know that it was all because she just wanted
to kiss David. And that was it.

She would have burned up with shame if not for one
thing. The way he reacted to her kiss.

He did not push her away or turn her aside with plat-
itudes about their friendship. Instead, he caught her close
to him and returned the kiss with heated ardor. Emily
might just be a Society miss still on the Marriage Mart,
but she had an outspoken artist for a sister-in-law and
she had lived almost all her life on a farm, and she was
aware of things other unmarried ladies her age were not.
She knew that David had wanted her last night, in a
physical way.

Maybe it was only the excitement of their schemes
that inflamed their passions. Or the memory of their old
friendship. Or maybe it was something entirely new,
something terrifying and strange and grand.

She had finally become so confused last night, her
mind dashing from one bizarre thought to another, that
she finally had to do *something*. She got out of bed and
made her way up to the attics to peer into Damien's old
trunk and cases one more time. Perhaps there was something in there to tell her more about the Star, something
she missed in her first hurried examination.

All she found, of course, was the detritus of a life ill-
lived. His traveling trunk was full of old gaming mark-
ers and notes, used packs of cards, billets-doux
(including some from one of their neighbors at Fair Oak,
the married Lady Anders), a few love tokens of lace
handkerchiefs and ribbon garters, a case containing du-
eling pistols, a few velvet coats and silk cravats. The
only thing worth saving in there was a small portrait of

their parents. There was certainly nothing about the Star of India. It appeared that the receipt she had found before, detailing the making of the paste copy, was all there was. The whereabouts of the genuine Star, it seemed, would always be a mystery.

Yet how could David's curse ever be broken if it was never found!

Don't be silly, Emily, she told herself, shutting the trunk on her brother's dusty remnants. *There are no such things as curses.*

She pushed the trunk back against the wall, where it made a dull, hollow thud. The day was already peeking pale gray above the horizon when she climbed back into her bed. There she fell into an uneasy sleep, to dream of floating jewels grasped at by many-armed gods.

Now, as she paced the footpath, she wished there *were* such things as curses. She would put one on Damien now, wherever he was, for bringing them all to this.

She stabbed at the ground beneath her feet with the tip of her umbrella, nearly catching her hem in the process. As she started to pull the umbrella up, she heard a high, sweet voice call out, "Lady Emily! Good afternoon, Lady Emily!"

She turned to see Anjali hurrying toward her, her pale lilac-colored cloak and bonnet like a bright springtime flower in the dismal day. Close behind her, of course, was her father. David.

He lifted his hat and smiled at her, and Emily's heart lifted like Signor Lunardi's balloon. Curses, jewels— what were they? Nothing, surely, beside such a smile.

She gave them a smile of her own, and went forward to greet them, leaving her umbrella lodged upright in the middle of the pathway.

"Lady Anjali! Lord Darlinghurst! How lovely to see you today." She held her hand out to David and he bowed over it. His lips touched and lingered on her gloved fingers, not just brushing the air above them.

So improper, Emily thought gleefully, and would have giggled if she was not far too old for such things.

But it was not nearly as improper as kissing on terraces at balls. She was practically a scarlet woman.

Anjali tugged at Emily's pelisse, pulling her away from such scandalous and delightful musings. She smiled down at the girl, who said, "My new governess already has a cold, Lady Emily, so I do not have to do any lessons today."

Emily laughed. "You are a very fortunate young lady, indeed, Lady Anjali, to have a whole day free of lessons. But how do you intend to fill such long hours?"

The girl's pink lips pouted. "Papa says the air is too chilly for eating ices, so I do not know."

Emily pretended to consider this carefully. "Yes, it is a bit chilly. But perhaps not too much so for tea and cakes?"

Anjali brightened, her green eyes widening. "Indeed, Lady Emily! Tea and cakes sounds just the thing." She turned a beseeching gaze up to her father.

David's lips twitched, but he crossed his arms sternly and said, "Tea *after* exercise. Why don't you run down to the end of the pathway and back?"

Anjali shook her head doubtfully. "My governess said a lady never runs."

"Well, then, walk as fast as you can. Lady Emily and I will follow."

Apparently, Anjali found walking fast to be acceptable, for she nodded and spun around to take off down the path. David offered his arm to Emily and they strolled in Anjali's wake, following the beacon of her lilac cloak.

"I am sorry, Emily—I had to bring her," David said ruefully. He pulled up her umbrella with his free hand as they passed, tucking it beneath his arm. "She becomes quite restive by teatime if she does not have some sort of activity."

"That is quite all right. I like Anjali." Emily slid him a sly glance from beneath her lashes. "But perhaps you felt the need to bring a chaperone along today, to prevent wild ladies from leaping on you and kissing you."

David laughed, his tone full of humor, though the glance he gave her in return smoldered with quite a different spark. "Shall we hide back behind that tree, and see what trouble we can devise before our little chaperone comes back?"

Emily looked at the tree in question. She knew he was only teasing her, but still there was that kernel of temptation . . .

But, no. She shook her head hard, trying to bring herself back to her senses. Scarlet woman, indeed. "I fear we have trouble of quite another sort to devise first," she said quietly.

David nodded, a somber veil dropping over his teasing gaze. "Quite right, and not much time in which to devise it. Do you happen to know of any social arrangements the Innises might have this week?"

Emily brightened a bit. *Here* was a question she knew the answer to. "Yes. Lady Innis told Georgina they would be attending Mrs. Chamberlain-Woods's musicale tonight. Georgina is friends with the Chamberlain-Woodses—they own two of her paintings. I was planning to attend myself."

"Tonight, eh?" David mused. He stared ahead of them, at where Anjali had paused to inspect some newly planted flowers, but he did not appear to truly see her. His gaze was narrowed, faraway. "That does not leave us much time. But we must make the most of it."

"The most of it?" Despite the chilled day, Emily's fingers warmed with excitement or trepidation. "David, do you have some sort of plan?"

"I may have, Emily."

"Well! What is it? Tell me!"

But he just shook his head. "In India, I have a cousin named Nikhil. In many ways he is very like your brother Damien, always in a scrape of one sort or another. My grandmother quite despairs of him, and he had to go live at our family's home in the mountains last year after a particularly troublesome incident."

Emily frowned at him. Whyever was he telling her tales of his cousin, when they needed to find a way to switch the two false Stars? "Every family has at least one troublesome member, I am sure."

"Indeed they do, and Nikhil is ours. One of ours, anyway." He smiled down at her, his gaze clearing. "Poor Em—you wonder why I am speaking of this cousin now. You see, when we were young, Nikhil devised quite an ingenious way to help his sister retrieve a necklace that she had foolishly lost. You already have the copy, so it should be perfect. We just need the right time."

"Papa!" Anjali was hurrying back toward them. "I walked to the very end. Now may I have tea?"

David leaned close to Emily and whispered, "Can you cry off the musicale tonight? Stay home by yourself?"

"Yes, of course."

"Wonderful. I will send a note later, telling you what we must do."

Before Emily could question these odd instructions, Anjali reached them, bobbing up and down on the toes of her little kid half-boots. Her cheeks were pink from the exercise. "May I have tea now, Papa?"

"Of course, *shona-moni*," David answered, taking her small hand in his while keeping Emily on his other arm. "I would be happy to escort the two loveliest ladies in Town to tea. Where shall we go? Gunter's again?"

"Oh, yes, please, Papa!"

As they turned back in the direction of the carriage path where David's phaeton waited, Emily was struck by the thought that anyone looking at them would think that for all the world they were a family. A couple and their little daughter.

A family of jewel-switchers and crazy relatives, mayhap, but a family nonetheless. Despite everything, that thought made Emily smile.

David watched Emily and Anjali as they sipped at their tea and compared the virtues of almond cakes versus lemon. They laughed, especially Anjali when Emily told her tales about their childhood at Fair Oak and Combe Lodge. He had never seen his shy girl with such a gleam in her eyes before, or her cheeks like rosy little apples as she giggled. He did not know what had affected such a transformation. He had feared, on the day they first met at Gunter's, that Anjali did not care overmuch for Emily and her boisterous family. He knew she was wary of finding herself suddenly with a "new mama," and had been ever since her ayah suggested such a thing in Calcutta. Yet here she was, laughing and smiling, asking Emily avid questions about what life in the English countryside was like.

No, he did not know what had happened. But he was glad that it had—whatever it was. He did not think he had ever been so content as he was at this very moment. The newly emerged sunlight falling from the windows shimmered on Emily's hair, turning it to pure spun gold. Even the curve of her cheek glistened like a gold-veined marble statue, as she leaned forward to whisper a jest in Anjali's ear. His daughter's laughter rang out as notes of music.

This was perfection, indeed, to have the two most beautiful ladies in the world sitting right beside him.

Their conversation was only for the two of them at the moment, but every once in a while Emily would refill David's teacup from the large pot at her elbow and give him a smile, or Anjali would reach out to touch his hand. The afternoon, which had begun in chill, gray confusion, was turned to a treasure just because they were all together.

The nonsense about the false Stars—the curse and the missing real one—receded, leaving only this beautiful, fleeting instant. All those things would have to be faced, and solved, very soon. But not just now.

He had always insisted to his grandmother that he had no desire to marry again, and he had thought that was true. And it *was* true that he wanted no more dutiful unions as he had with Rupasri, the sort of bond that brought no heartache and some contentment, but little joy. The joy he had seen between his own passionately attached parents. Deep down, under all his restlessness, his resolve to live in devotion to his family and daughter, he had wanted such a thing for himself. Longed for it, even, in his darkest heart of hearts. But he knew that it did not exist for people such as him—it belonged only to the chosen few.

Now he saw that he was wrong. Very wrong. Such limitless joy sat right in front of him.

It would probably not last for long. Emily had many suitors, far more eligible than the "Indian earl." And he had his own future to face, with or without the Star. But for now, for this afternoon, he held perfection in his hands.

And it was more beautiful than even the shining blue facets of the Star could hope to be.

Chapter Twelve

"Oh, Em! You do seem pale." Georgina touched Emily's cheek gently with the back of her hand. Her dark red brows were furrowed in a concerned frown that even her fashionably low emerald bandeau could not hide. "And warm, too. I do hope you have not caught that fever that is going 'round. I knew you should not have gone walking this afternoon!"

Pricked by sharp, tiny needles of guilt over her deception, Emily reached up and caught Georgina's hand in her own. "I am sure I haven't caught a chill, Georgie. It is just a bit of a cold and will surely be gone by tomorrow. I only need a good night's sleep and some of Cook's beef tea."

Georgina seemed unconvinced. "Yes. Of course you must stay home and rest—there is no question of your attending the musicale. Perhaps I should stay here with you."

"No!" Emily cried out. Then, seeing the startled expression on Georgina's face, she carefully lowered her voice back to a hoarse whisper. "No, Georgie, I know how you have been looking forward to seeing Mrs. Chamberlain-Woods again and talking about art with her. Even Alex was saying—"

She was interrupted by a quick tap at her door, and

then her brother stuck his head in. Like Georgina, he was already dressed for the evening. Even the usually unruly waves of his dark hair were smoothed into a stylish Brutus.

"What is this? Did I hear my name?" he said, with a grin.

"Yes, I was just saying that Georgina *must* go to the musicale with you tonight," Emily answered. "Even you said you were looking forward to it, Alex, and you so seldom look forward to any social occasion."

"And I said I should stay home with Emily and keep an eye on her," Georgina said stubbornly. "Colds can be quite dangerous, particularly at this time of year."

"And I have said there is no need," insisted Emily. "I am just going to sleep, and I would feel wretched if I ruined everyone's evening."

"Nonsense, Em," Alex said. "I *do* enjoy some music when it is well played, as it generally is at Mrs. Chamberlain-Woods'. But I have no objection to a quiet evening at home, especially when you are ill, Buttercup. Perhaps we should both stay here with you."

"No, no," Emily protested. She could feel the whole situation sliding out of her grasp, like a wet length of rope, and she grasped at it desperately. If they did *not* leave, if they insisted on staying to play nursemaid to her, she would never be able to slip out of the house and meet David behind the mews. Even if she feigned sleep, they would be peeking in at her every half-hour, quite as if she was little Elizabeth Anne's age.

Relatives, as beloved as they were, could be exasperating at times.

"You two must go," she said, sliding back down her pillows and trying to appear exhausted and in need of solitude. "Mrs. Chamberlain-Woods is expecting you— you are no doubt to be the stars of her soiree. And there will be so many people wanting to speak with you about your paintings, Georgie."

Georgina wavered, glancing back at her husband, who shrugged. It was obvious that she wanted to go out and talk about her art, but she also wanted to stay home. "I am not sure . . ."

"Please," Emily begged. "I would not be able to rest easy if I knew I kept you from the musicale."

Georgina finally nodded. "Very well. We will go, then, but we will be back early. If you are still unwell, I shall send for the physician."

"All right, Georgie," Emily answered. After all, by the time they returned she would be sleeping peacefully. But if they *did* come home early, she and David would have to work quickly. "Go now, and have a fine time."

Georgina kissed Emily's brow, and hurried out in a flurry of emerald green silk. Alex also came in to kiss her. As his lips brushed her cheek, he whispered, "Enjoy your evening of peace and quiet, Em. I will keep her out for as long as I can."

Emily smiled up at him. "I love you, Alex. You are the best of brothers."

"And you are quite satisfactory as a sister."

"Even if I do not do my duty and settle on a suitable betrothal?"

"Em, you would be the best of sisters if you sat on the highest shelf for a hundred years. But I do not think it will come to that, do you? I did hear that you were having a fine afternoon at the British Museum the other day." He winked at her. "I expect a call from Lord Darlinghurst any day now."

Emily felt her face flame as brightly as the fire now crackling in her grate. She sank back under the bedclothes. "Good night, Alex!"

"Good night, Em."

From through the layers of linens, Emily heard the

door close and a brief clamor on the landing as Georgina and Alex put on their wraps and kissed their children good-night. After several minutes, there was the sound of the carriage clattering away down the street.

Alone at last!

Emily tossed back the blankets and sat up to peer at the ormolu clock on the mantel. It was very nearly time for her to meet David—and for them to commence whatever plan he had devised.

Her stomach was in such knots! She had never been as painfully proper as many of the young ladies with whom she made her curtsy to the queen three years ago—young ladies who were now married to painfully proper young men, with proper little babies in their nurseries. She had always thought nothing of talking about farming theories at a ball, or riding faster than was customary down Rotten Row, or even driving her sister-in-law's phaeton.

But she had never thought of sneaking out of the house in the night!

"There is a first time for everything, Emily," she told herself. "Boudicca never would have defeated the Romans if she was too chickenhearted to leave her chamber."

Besides—what would David think of her if she backed out now?

Newly resolved, Emily stood up and threw off her dressing gown. Beneath it, she wore clothes purloined from Damien's trunk—dark trousers and jacket over a soft cambric shirt, clothes he wore before dissipation made him bloated. Unlike Alex, who was tall and solidly muscled, Damien had always been shorter. His garments fit her well enough, and, when wearing her riding boots and with her pale hair concealed beneath a black hat, she could pass for a lad. From a distance. In faint light. Maybe.

Well, at least she could move more freely than in a gown and petticoats. It even felt rather nice, she thought, taking a few experimental strides around the room. She was tempted to jump about, just because she could, but there was no time. She had to meet David. She made a round-shaped log out of pillows beneath her bed-clothes—that should fool her maid, if she peeked in on Emily. Becky would never dare to try to wake her. After slipping the new-made Star into her coat pocket and pulling on dark gloves, she slid out of her room and down the staircase, keeping carefully to the shadows.

The house was silent in the wake of the duke and duchess's departure, all the servants gone off to other, quieter duties. The only light was from one candelabrum in the foyer, making it easy—too easy?—for her to ease out of the front door. She crept around to the back garden and down to the mews, where David's note had instructed her to wait for him.

There appeared to be no one about. The area was deserted, silent beneath the moon and stars and the cool evening wind.

Why had she never noticed before how very silent the neighborhood was after dark? Emily shivered a bit, pulling her borrowed coat closer about her. She could almost be the only person in the whole city.

Yet even as she thought this, strong hands grasped her shoulders and spun her about. She opened her lips to scream—only to have the sound caught by a kiss.

A rather familiar-feeling kiss. And a familiar, delicious scent of sandalwood soap surrounded her. Her shriek turned into a soft moan, and she reached up to clasp David around the neck. His skin was hot through the thin leather of her gloves.

She was just beginning to lose herself in that embrace when he pulled away, grinning down at her in the moonlight. "I must say, Lady Emily, you look very fetching in breeches," he whispered in her ear.

His hands clasped her waist loosely as she leaned back to gaze up at him. He did not look like himself this evening—not like the David she had come to know, in his stylish coats and waistcoats, his perfectly tied cravats. Tonight, he wore a strange costume of loose black cotton trousers with a black tunic and long waistcoat. His hair was concealed by the folds of an exotic black turban. The gleam of a dagger could just be seen peering from the folds of his sash.

"You look quite—*fetching* yourself," she murmured. In truth, if he had a gold earring he could pass for a Barbary pirate.

He laughed, his teeth very white against all that black. "I am sure I look like a murderous *thuggee,* but none of my other clothes allow such concealment. Now, come— we have to hurry. The Innises have left for the musicale, but who knows how long they will be gone. We must be well away before they return."

"And before Georgina and Alex get back and insist on checking on my 'fever,' " Emily answered. She took his hand and followed him onto the back street heading away from the mews. "But what will we do once we get to the Innises' house?"

"My dear Boudicca, don't you know? We are going to break in and exchange one false Star for another. Isn't that what you've been secretly planning all along?"

Exchange one Star for the other. It sounded so very simple, Emily thought. It was just too bad that the execution did not prove to be so easy.

Execution. Now, *there* was a word. Surely that was what awaited them if they were caught in this scheme. She and David would be dead or in Australia. Anjali would be parentless and Georgina and Alex would be in despair.

But somehow, even with all that lurking above her, Emily felt alive with excitement. This was what she had been missing in all those ballrooms—missing ever since she and David last dashed across the summer fields at Fair Oak. She had been missing *life*.

If only she could have found it some other way, she mused wryly. In dancing, perhaps, or needlework, rather than breaking and entering. But they would not be caught. They would retrieve the paste Star and be gone from here.

She hoped.

David held her up to the library window at the Innis house, the balls of her feet balanced in his palms as she clung to the cold marble ledge with her gloved fingers. It was pitch black in there, a ray of errant moonlight just catching on the Star's glass case.

"Well?" David asked. "Can you see anything?" He did not even sound breathless from the effort of holding her aloft.

But Emily was not sure how long she could keep her balance. "Not a thing," she said, wobbling against the wall. "There is no one there. I can see the case, but I do not know if it still contains the Star."

"Is the window locked?"

The glass was an old-fashioned casement, unusual for a couple with such modern sensibilities as the Innises. Perhaps they had just not yet gotten around to replacing them, which made Emily's task easier. It was fairly simple to slip her thin wire between the panes and pop up the latch. She pushed open the window and answered, "Not anymore."

"Excellent." David hoisted her up even further, until she could pull herself up into the room. She tumbled to the floor with a deafening (to her ears, anyway) thud.

She lay there on the carpet, breath held as she listened for running feet and warning shouts. Nothing. Only silence.

Her breath left her lungs in a great *whoosh,* and she sat up and turned back toward the window. David's hands, also encased in dark leather gloves, appeared over the ledge and he hoisted himself up and over. Unlike her own ignominious fall, he landed lightly on his feet, like an Indian panther.

He clasped her hands and drew her off the carpet. "All right?" he whispered.

Emily nodded mutely, and turned in the direction of the glass case. As if in a trance, she moved across the library, dodging the dark shapes of chairs and desks and settees, with David close behind her.

This has to be a dream, she thought. Only David's hand in hers was real.

She stopped at the glass case, staring down at it. The Star *was* there, winking and sparkling up at her as if to mock her endeavors. She pressed her fingertips against the lock, suddenly realizing she had lost her wire.

"Looking for this?" David pressed the thin silver length into her palm. "You dropped it on the carpet."

Emily nodded, still silent. She turned the wire over in her hand, staring at the lock.

David's hands landed lightly at her waist, a warm, reassuring pressure. "You can do this, Boudicca."

Could she? It was true that once she had been quite shamefully proficient at picking locks. The blacksmith's apprentice at Fair Oak had taught her, and she had used the skill to break into Damien's strong box on his infrequent visits to Fair Oak. The few coins she took were never enough for him to notice, but they meant extra seed or a leak in the roof patched to Emily.

That was years ago, though. She had not tried it since.

She flexed her fingers and closed her eyes, trying to remember just the right twist to make the lock open to her.

Steadied by David's nearness, she opened her eyes. Slowly, carefully, she slid the end of the wire into the tiny opening of the lock. She wiggled it around, trying to get it just under the mechanism. She only just felt it, when the library door gave an ominous click behind them. The faint echo of voices, a giggle, came to their ears in the darkness.

"Blast!" Emily cursed under her breath, yanking the wire out of the lock. They were caught!

"Come with me," David muttered. He pulled her across the room, and reached out to draw open the door of a cupboard. It appeared to be a section of a bookcase, tucked into a corner, but Emily saw it was in reality a tiny closet, with banks of crates pushed against the walls. She had only a fleeting glimpse before she threw herself inside, pressing back against the crates.

David slid in beside her, drawing the door shut just as candlelight spilled into the library—across the glass case where they had been standing only an instant before.

David left the closet door open a crack. Emily peered through it, her hand braced against the wall and a prayer of thanksgiving whispering in her mind.

A footman, his powdered wig askew and the jacket of his livery unbuttoned, appeared in the library, a branch of candles in his hand. He was closely followed by a girl in a housemaid's black dress and white apron. Her cap was gone, her light brown hair spilling over her shoulders.

Surely they have not come here to clean, Emily thought.

Her suspicions were quite confirmed when the footman placed the light down on the desk and drew the maid into his arms.

"Ooh, Johnny!" the girl squealed. "Yer ever so naughty."

The footman's hand slid down to her backside and squeezed, as he lowered his head to kiss her neck. "I can be even naughtier, Nell, you just watch!"

Nell squealed again, and dissolved into giggles as he proceeded to pull up her black skirts. "We'll be caught! And I'll be sacked for sure. So will you."

"And who's to catch us?" Johnny's voice was muffled in Nell's bosom. "Mr. Hudson and Mrs. Barnes are snoring away, and the master and mistress won't be home for hours. Plenty of time for a bit of fun, eh, Nell?"

Nell went into a paroxysm of laughter as Johnny tipped her back onto a settee. They were mercifully hidden from Emily's view by the furniture's brocade back, but she had to draw the closet door shut when she saw a pair of satin livery breeches and a white petticoat go sailing down to the carpet.

She was quite afraid she was going to have a fit of the giggles herself. She was shaking with the force of her nerves at having her lock-picking interrupted by such, er, lively activity, and hysterical laughter lurked just below the surface.

Fortunately, the cupboard was quite soundproof once closed, and she didn't have to hear any more of Nell's squeals. Unfortunately, all the light was also gone, and the heavy darkness pressed in upon her.

She took a deep breath—and inhaled David's sandalwood scent. Suddenly, the darkness did not seem quite so frightening. His presence was all around her, even though she could not see him, and she had a new fear—that he would touch her, and she would start gasping and giggling just like Nell.

"Are you all right, Em?" he murmured. His voice enfolded her, like a thick velvet coverlet, wrapping about her, drawing her in.

She felt one of the crates at the back of her knees, and sank down onto it, reaching up to pull off her hat and shake her hair free. "Yes. Quite all right." Her voice was hoarse and trembling, but hopefully he would put that down to her shock at being interrupted. Not at the sudden, drugging warmth that flooded her veins and made her weak and slow.

Through the door, a sudden high-pitched scream could be heard. "Ooh, Johnny! Yer ever so big. I don't think as how it'll fit."

Emily choked on a snicker, and pressed her hand to her mouth.

"Well," David drawled, laughter rich in his voice. "I do not suppose we will be free of this hidey-hole any time soon. Not if young Johnny's, er, attributes continue to be as alluring to Nell as they are at present."

Emily moved her hands to cover her whole face, forgetting for an instant that it was completely dark in their closet and he could not see her scarlet cheeks. "Um—no. I daresay you are right. You should sit down, David."

"Where?"

Here, and then I'll sit on your lap and pretend we are Johnny and Nell, Emily thought, then almost slapped herself for such unladylike thoughts. But she could not deny that, for a moment, she had wished she was a housemaid and not a duke's sister.

"There is a crate here beside mine," she said. "They seem quite solid."

She felt the brush of cool air as he moved to sit on the crate behind hers, the caress of muslin cloth on her wrist. She started as his hands found her in the dark, sliding around her waist to draw her close.

For a second, she held herself stiffly, unyielding, scared to let herself give in for fear of what she might do. But the darkness was seductive, urging her to give in to his touch, to let herself be free for just a while. Not as free as Nell, of course, but still . . .

She relaxed against David, letting her head drop back

to rest against his chest. She felt his chin nestle atop her head, his breath stirring her hair. Her hands slid atop his, and they sat there for a few moments, entwined, silent.

Then a long moan broke across the quiet, and Emily knew she had to speak, to cover the noise from Johnny and Nell, or she would go mad.

"David, talk to me," she urged.

"What would you like to talk about?" he said, his voice heavy and rich, like chocolate or sweet brandy.

"Oh—a tale of India. That would be appropriate, I think."

"You probably know more than I do, with all of the reading you have done."

"Of course I do not. You have lived there; you know the sights and scents and feelings. I can only imagine them." And that had been all she had done in her life— imagined. Until now. Here, in this dark little closet, she felt that all the mysteries of life, love, and death could be revealed to her. All in David's voice and touch.

After a long second of silence, he said, "I can tell you a tale of the Star. My grandmother told it to me when I was young."

"Oh, yes! Please tell me, David."

When he began his tale, his cultured London accent fell away, his tones became lilting and musical, touched with the spice and heaviness of his home. "There was once a prince who lived in ancient India. His name was Krishna, and he was an incarnation of the god Vishnu. He founded the city of Dwarka, on the coast of the land of Gujarat before it fell into the sea and disappeared. Some say it was the true Atlantis."

Emily closed her eyes, and she could see it, the shining city by the sea. It made everything—the darkness, the breaking and entering, Nell and Johnny—recede away.

David went on. "In Dwarka lived a man named Sattrajit who worshipped Surya—the sun. One day, while Sattrajit was walking on the shore, Surya appeared before him and rewarded his devotion with a jewel. This jewel, as brilliant as the sea itself, brought great prosperity to the city, and kept away all evil—even thieves and famine and plague."

"The Star?"

"Perhaps. But Sattrajit feared that Krishna would demand the jewel, so he gave it to his brother Prasena. But, you see, the jewel would only do good for the good man—and bad for the bad man."

"And Prasena was bad?"

"Indeed. He went out hunting, and was killed by the king of bears, who took the jewel to a cave."

Emily was fascinated. "Then what happened?"

"When people found Prasena dead, they said that Krishna killed him for the stone. To prove his innocence, Krishna found the king of bears in his cave and fought him for twenty-one days, until the bear gave up the jewel. When Krishna returned with it, people believed he was innocent after all. Then he gave it away to a virtuous maiden—and eventually it ended up in a great temple."

His voice stilled. Emily's eyes opened, and she was half-surprised to find herself still in the dark closet and not in the cave of the king of bears. "Was that all?"

David gave a low, rumbling laugh. "Of course not. Such tales go on forever in India. The stone passes from hand to hand, some worthy, many not. Krishna could not keep it himself, you see, because he had sixteen thousand wives, and that was hardly virtuous."

Emily laughed. "Sixteen thousand!"

"Yes. One can only hope that they were all as happy as Nell out there."

Emily laughed even harder, so hard that she was

afraid she could never stop. She muffled the sound behind her hand.

"It is said," David continued, his clasp on her tightening, "that whoever possesses the jewel moves like the sun, wearing a garland of light."

"Then it should be easy to find the Star! We need only look for the person wearing a garland of light."

David's voice, so full of laughter only a moment before, was suddenly very serious. "I would say that was you, Emily. You are the garland of light. My *shona*—my gold."

Emily's own laughter died away. She turned in his arms, staring up at him. She could not see his face—she could only feel him, sense him. "Why did you come back from India after all these years?"

"I thought it was to see my father's home again, to take my daughter away from people scheming to marry her off when she is just a child. And I do want those things. But I think that the truth is—I came back to find you again."

Emily's throat was thick with unshed tears; her eyes itched with them. This was frightening. More frightening than picking that lock. More frightening than being left alone to tend Fair Oak and her mother. More frightening than anything ever. She could feel pieces of the cocoon with which she had surrounded herself for years chipping and falling away, leaving her naked and vulnerable.

But surely David was worth it. She had been waiting for him since she was a child—since before she was born, even. She was meant for him, and he for her.

But how could something that was meant to be be so scary?

Be brave, she urged herself. It was never more important than now. She leaned against him, her lips finding his in the darkness. They met and clung, their breath mingled, and it was perfect—like a garland of light. His hands drew her across his lap, and she gasped in purest pleasure. This was where she belonged.

When they parted, she buried her face against the curve of his throat. "I am glad you came back, whatever the reason," she whispered. "For, if you had not, I would have had to go to India myself to find you."

He held her close, their hearts beating together. "*Ami tomake bhalobashi,*" he said, kissing her hair, her temple, her cheek.

Emily did not ask what that meant—she already knew, in her heart. And her heart whispered back in kind, *I love you.*

It could have been only moments later, or hours, when Emily felt David stir. Only then did she notice that Johnny and Nell were silent, the thin line of light from their candles gone from beneath the door.

Apparently, the amorous pair had concluded their business and gone back to their duties—which meant that Sir Charles and Lady Innis must surely be returning home very soon.

Emily was still sitting with her head resting on David's shoulder. They had not spoken for a long while, just sat together in sweet silence, surrounded by the echoes of their breathing and heartbeats.

She could have stayed like that forever, were it not for the fact that they were illegally in someone else's home, hiding out in a tiny library closet. They had very nearly been caught breaking into the case, and they were not out of danger yet. The jewels still had to be switched, and she had to be home in her bed before Alex and Georgina returned.

But still, despite all of that, this had been a lovely night—one she would not have traded for anything.

She lifted her head from David's shoulder, staring at

the absence of light from beneath the door. "It seems our friends Johnny and Nell have departed," she murmured.

"Indeed it does," David answered. She felt him smooth her hair back from her face, his touch tender. "We should conclude our errand before the owners of the house return. Unless we could take a page from Johnny and Nell's book, and convince them we are just a pair of vagabonds searching for a likely spot for a tryst."

Emily gave a choked giggle. "I somehow doubt that would work! They do know us, you remember, though perhaps not in our current guises."

"Ah, well. No doubt you are right. It might have been amusing to try, though." David gently moved her aside, and she sensed him standing up in the gloom. There was a soft click, and the closet door opened, letting in the glow of moonlight.

"It appears we are alone," he whispered. "Come, my Boudicca, we should complete our errand and depart."

Emily nodded, and reached out to take his hand. His fingers entwined with hers, warm and reassuring even through their gloves. He led her into the library, which suddenly seemed vast after their tiny hiding place, to the waiting glass case.

Amazingly, it looked just the same as it had before they were so rudely interrupted. Somehow, she expected the whole world to have changed, just because her own heart was transformed.

She took out the wire again and fit it back into the lock. It had bent when she stuck it into her pocket, though, and would not easily maneuver into place. Emily bit her lip, twisting at it with her fingertips. In the corner, a tall clock tolled the hour in stentorian tones. She started, the wire slipping through her fingers.

Midnight, she thought, as the last bell echoed away. *The witching hour. How very appropriate.*

"It is just the clock, Em," David said reassuringly. "Everything is fine."

"Yes," she answered. She slid the wire in once again, and this time she felt the tiny locking mechanism pop free. She pulled open the case and reached in to clasp the paste Star, her breath suspended. She half-expected bells and whistles to explode in the room, bringing the entire household at a run. She quickly placed the stone securely inside her coat.

But there was nothing. Only the thick silence of the night. Swiftly, her hands trembling, she took out Mr. Jervis's sapphire and placed it carefully on the satin-swathed platform. It twinkled there in a bar of starlight.

Perfect. She closed up the case and clicked the lock back into place.

"It is done," she whispered.

"Then, let us depart." David clasped her arm and led her toward the half-open window. They were only a few feet away when there was a sudden burst of noise from outside the library.

"I trust your evening was enjoyable, sir," a man said, in a butler's deep, mannered tones. At least it was not young Johnny.

Emily froze, as if by standing very, very still she could disappear.

"It was, until that Miss Freeman insisted on playing the harp, Hudson," Sir Charles Innis replied. "I vow I heard all the dogs on the street howling."

"Oh, my dear, it was not that bad," chided Lady Innis, with the crisp rustle of satin, as if she was shedding her evening cloak. "She had great—enthusiasm for the music."

"Enthusiasm! Is that what they are calling it now?"

"I enjoyed it. Are you going to retire now, my dear?"

"No, no, Alice. You go on. I want to finish some paperwork in the library first."

Lady Innis laughed. "You mean you want to stare at the Star one more time."

David tugged at Emily's arm, pulling her toward the window. She bumped into a chair, and felt the wire fall from her hand onto the carpet. There was no time to retrieve it, though—the knob of the library door was turning.

David shoved open the window, and lifted Emily up to drop her unceremoniously out of it.

"Oof!" she gasped, as she landed in an untidy heap on the grass. She crawled beneath a nearby bush just as David slid out of the casement behind her, as lithe as the jungle cat she had imagined him earlier. He landed silently on the balls of his feet, and ducked down to join her under the bush just as a bellow echoed from the library.

"An open window!" Sir Charles shouted. "How often must I tell those dratted servants how bad the night air is for my artifacts? I won't allow them in my library in the future!"

The window slammed shut. Emily feared she would again burst into hysterical laughter, and lowered her head to the grass to stifle it. "It is a very good thing Sir Charles does not know what else his servants are up to in the library."

"I should say not," David muttered, laughter at the edges of his words. "Come, we need to be away from here."

Clasping hands, they crawled from beneath the sheltering bush and dashed across the small garden. Emily glanced back as David boosted her over the wall. Every window of the library blazed with light now, but there was no alarm raised. The only sound was that of night birds in their trees, and her own labored breathing. It had been years since she ran so freely over the countryside, and this dash through the city streets made her limbs ache. She paused at the edge of her own street to press her hand to her side, trying to calm her pounding heart.

David, she noticed, appeared as if he had only been out for a summer stroll. He stopped beside her, his own breath only slightly quickened.

Emily leaned against a fence rail that sheltered the servants' entrance many feet below. She studied David in the light of the waning moon and stars. He seemed an exotic, nighttime mirage, dark and remote, like the god who coveted the jewel and fought a bear for it. Had he really held her in his arms, and whispered such achingly sweet words? Words she had waited a lifetime to hear?

He reached up and pulled the turban from his head, ruffling his black hair. It fell over his brow like satin commas, and Emily could not help herself—she reached up to sweep them back, the strands catching at her fingers like stray silk.

He grinned down at her. "We did it, Em. It is finished."

She smiled doubtfully. Yes, it was finished. She had what she wanted. Her family was safe. But was his?

The true Star of India was still out there somewhere.

"Yes, we did it!" she said, some of the cold doubt falling away in a sudden rush of exhilaration. "I can scarce believe it." She threw her arms around him, and felt him lift her from her feet. He twirled her around until the night sky tilted tipsily above her, and she laughed, giddy with delight. "I could not have done it without you."

"It was glorious fun, Em," he answered, lowering her slowly to her feet. "I haven't felt like that since we were children."

"Well, we shall just have to find other sources of fun, since I do not think I could survive burgling every night. Not to mention running through the London streets!" She paused, and reached up to gently cradle his cheek in her palm. "I have to admit, though—it *was* glorious. I will always remember it."

David turned his head to press a lingering kiss into her hand. "So will I. But I should be going home now, and you should find your bed before your brother and his wife return."

Alex and Georgina! How could she have ever forgotten them? They would be home at any moment, and expected to find her ill in her chamber. Georgina was daring, but not even she would understand midnight thievery.

"Of course," she said, and went up on tiptoe to kiss his cheek. "Shall we meet again soon? I confess I am quite eager to hear more of your cousin's adventure with that stolen necklace—the one that inspired our little plan tonight."

"Oh, yes. Nikhil's necklace." David smiled at her, and slowly backed away from her embrace. "I would be happy to tell you of it one day. And I am sure we will meet again. Good night, Emily."

With that, he melted into the shadows, leaving Emily alone. She suddenly noticed how chill the evening air had become; it danced over her neck and arms, raising goosebumps. She stood there for a long moment, staring at the spot where David had stood. But she could still sense his gaze, watching her from the darkness.

Only the rattle of carriage wheels broke her strange reverie. She glanced back over her shoulder to see that it was her brother's equipage, returned from the musicale, coming inexorably toward her.

"Blast!" Emily cursed. How could she have gotten through all the other dangers of the evening, only to be caught by her own silly daydreaming? She ducked her head and ran as fast as she could along behind the houses. Praying that she would not run into any more stray servants, she dashed up the back stairs, pulling off her hat and coat as she went.

She scarcely had time to thrust her borrowed clothes beneath the bed, pull on her dressing gown, and dive beneath the bedclothes. She squeezed her eyes shut and struggled to control her breathing. Her door clicked open softly, and she heard Georgina whisper, "She is asleep. Poor Emily! Such a grand party she missed."

Emily smiled secretly into her pillow. A grand party, indeed—if only they knew.

Chapter Thirteen

"*I* am glad you are feeling more the thing this morning, Emily," Georgina said, as she passed a cup of chocolate across the breakfast table to Emily. "It is too bad you missed the musicale last night, but now you can go with me to the mantua-maker this afternoon. There is a new peach-colored muslin there I think you will like."

"I was also sorry to miss the musicale," Emily answered. She took the cup, and reached for the rack of toast, despite the fact that she had already eaten three slices. Somehow, she had an uncommon appetite this morning. "I always thoroughly enjoy seeing Mrs. Chamberlain-Woods."

"Do not be too sorry, Em," Alex said, turning the page of his newspaper. "Miss Freeman was there with her dreaded harp."

Emily laughed. "Oh, yes! I heard that all the dogs on the street commenced howling when she . . ." She broke off, suddenly recalling where exactly she had heard that little snippet. From Sir Charles Innis, while she hid in his library.

Georgina gave her a puzzled glance. "Where did you hear such a thing, Emily? The musicale only occurred last night, surely it is too early for such gossip to be spreading."

"I—must have read it. In one of the papers. They are so quick with tittle-tattle, you know." She tapped at the paper folded up beside her plate.

"Oh, that one!" Georgina said, with a dismissive little wave of her hand. "It is full of nothing but scurrilous gossip. I am sure no dogs howled at all during Miss Freeman's, er, most lovely performance. Don't you agree, Alex darling?"

"Oh, indeed, my dear," Alex said. "I do believe it was a cat that was howling."

"Oh, you!" Georgina cried, laughing as she swatted playfully at her husband's arm. "Very well, so Miss Freeman's performance does not seem to improve no matter how many years she practices or how many music masters her father hires. But the rest of the performances were quite fine—there was even the soprano Madame Cascatti from Drury Lane. Poor Em—how tiresome it must have been to spend the whole night at home feeling miserable!"

"Yes," Emily murmured, concentrating very hard on her plate of eggs and kippers and toast. "Tiresome indeed."

"Here is an article you might find interesting, Em," Alex said. "Gemological scholars are coming today to inspect the Star of India at the home of Sir Charles Innis, and by tomorrow it will be on its way to the Mercer Museum."

Emily's gaze snapped up from her eggs. "Indeed? Today? That is quite—sudden." And quite fortunate that she had taken care of matters last night and not tarried.

"Yes, but of course the museum is very eager to take possession. It should herald many new donations to their coffers." Alex folded the newspaper and tucked it beneath his plate. "It is too bad that Damien lost the stone to Innis so long ago, and that we were unable to fulfill our obligation to Lord Darlinghurst. I did try to purchase it back from Innis, but he was insistent that it go to the museum. And, I suppose, it is truly the best place for it."

Emily stared at her brother, startled and incredulous. "You *knew* the story of the Star's loss, Alex? About how foolish Damien was?"

"Of course. Mother told me, not long after I returned home from Spain. She did not know then who exactly had bought the Star, though, and did not find out until years later. It is a damnable thing, truly." He frowned fiercely down at the paper. "I have tried to set all of Damien's wrongs right, but that one will never be remedied."

"Yes," Emily whispered. "I know exactly what you mean."

"Oh, Em." Alex reached out to squeeze her hand, giving her a rueful smile. "You have been hurt more than anyone by our brother's vices. You must not worry about it any longer. It is in the past."

"It *is* a most unfortunate situation," Georgina said. "But I think Lord Darlinghurst would rather have *another* jewel from our family. One far more valuable than any sapphire could ever be."

Alex grinned. "I think you are absolutely right, darling."

Emily suddenly felt a bit queasy. All of the chocolate, toast, and eggs she had consumed sat uneasily in her stomach with all this talk of jewels and families, and their two stares on her. "I—hm. Excuse me, please, Alex, Georgie."

"Are you quite all right, Emily?" Georgina asked in a concerned tone. "Is your fever returning?"

"No, I am well. I just must— Excuse me." Emily pushed herself back from the table and hurried out of the breakfast room.

"Oh, Alex, you should not have teased her so about

Lord Darlinghurst," she heard Georgina chide her brother.

"I, tease her? What about you, my lady wife? You are constantly asking her about her suitors!"

Emily shook her head, and turned to go up the staircase to her own chamber. As she placed her foot on the first step, she heard the butler call, "Lady Emily. This package just came for you."

"Thank you, Greene," Emily said, accepting the small, flat box wrapped in brightly striped paper.

She turned it over in her hand, puzzled. It did not rattle or rustle, and she was not expecting any deliveries today. She sometimes received flowers from various suitors, of course, but that was all. And this was obviously not flowers.

Emily tucked the box beneath her arm and carried it up to her bedroom where she could open it in private. She climbed up onto the high bed and carefully folded back the paper to find a plain wooden case.

It did not appear dangerous in any way, but she was still a bit jumpy after all the excitement of the night before. With a little laugh at herself, she opened the top—and her laughter faded away.

There, nestled on dark red velvet, were the necklace and earrings she had traded for the new Star at Mr. Jervis's shop. The delicate web of pearls and diamonds that had been Alex and Georgina's gift to her on her last birthday twinkled. It had pained her so to give them up, but she had pushed that down deep under necessity—as she had been doing for years. Seeing them there now, returned to her, she felt a great lump rise in her throat.

Emily took them out of the box, spreading their sparkle across the satin counterpane. As she fastened the earrings to her lobes, she saw the glint of something else in the case. She reached in and pulled out the wire she

had dropped the night before. Wrapped about its thin
length, tied with a small red ribbon, was a piece of paper.

Grinning helplessly, Emily pulled it off and smoothed
it across her lap to read.

*My dear Boudicca—I hope you never have need of
this little wire again, but just in case (for one never
knows what awaits in life) I am returning it to you.
I am also returning something else which I believe
belongs to you. It took a great deal of time to persuade Mr. Jervis to show me which pieces were
yours, but it will be worth it to see them around
your neck and in your ears when next we dance at
a ball.*

*Perhaps you would care to join Anjali and my-
self at Astley's Amphitheatre next week? Or, if elephants and acrobats hold no excitement for you, tea
again.*

Sincerely, your friend, David Huntington

Emily pressed her hand to her mouth. So, last night
had not been some sort of dream. His caresses, his sweet
words, were real and true. As real as these jewels that
sparkled before her.

If only she had a gift half so fine to give him in return.

There was a quick knock at the door, and Emily
hastily thrust the note and wire under a cushion. "Come
in," she called.

Georgina stuck her head into the room. "I just wanted
to look in on you, Emily dear, to be sure you are not ill
again."

Emily smiled at her. "I am well, truly, Georgie."

"Yes, I can see that. You have not smiled so in days."
She came into the chamber to perch on the edge of the
bed beside Emily. "Oh, I see your birthday jewels are
back from being cleaned!"

Cleaned? Oh, yes—now Emily remembered her ear-lier deception about the gems' disappearance. "They just arrived."

"Hm. They do look beautiful, I must say. So sparkling and fresh. Perhaps I should have my emeralds cleaned. But, really, I just wanted to tell you, Emily, that . . ."

Her words were suddenly drowned out by a tumult in the corridor. There was a strange banging noise, and raised voices. Georgina hurried to the door, with Emily close behind.

A procession of footmen were making their way to the staircase, laden with baskets and cases. One of them had just run into the wall with the edge of a trunk, leav-ing streaks of dust on the silk wallpaper.

Emily recognized that trunk—she had taken clothes out of it just the day before. It was Damien's. But where was it going?

"What is amiss, Greene?" Georgina asked the butler, who was interrupted in the middle of a brisk scold to the young footman.

"I beg your pardon, Your Grace," he said. "We were just taking away the cases, as you instructed, when Tim-othy lost control of the trunk. I fear the trunk was far too wide for the servants' staircase, or we should never have disturbed you, Your Grace."

"I am ever so sorry, Your Grace," young Timothy stammered. "But this here trunk isn't as heavy as it ap-pears, and I used too much force when I hefted it. It's very light for its size."

"Quite all right," Georgina said reassuringly. "Carry on, please, but carefully."

"What is happening, Georgie?" Emily asked, staring after the vanishing luggage.

"Nothing to worry about, Em. It is just that all this fuss about the Star reminded me of all the things your late brother left in the attics. And Greene complained of some strange noises there, as if mice had gotten in amongst all the clutter. We do not want mice, or Damien's belongings, in our lives any longer, so I instructed Greene to dispose of them."

"Yes," Emily muttered. "Quite right, Georgie. No mice." She was distracted by the way Timothy the footman was able to carry the large trunk on one shoulder. *Isn't as heavy as it appears*—she suddenly remembered the hollow thud the trunk had made as she pushed it back against the wall.

"Wait!" she cried out. "Bring the trunk back. Put it here in my chamber."

"Emily," Georgina protested. "You do not want that dusty thing in your room. It will just bring up old memories."

"Do not worry, Georgie," Emily reassured her. "I just want to go through it, then you may toss it out to your heart's content."

Georgina gave her a worried glance. "Emily," she said quietly. "I do not think it is such a fine idea for you to recall—well, such old occurrences. It is best to let such things go, to look only to the future. Believe me, I know this. There is much in my own past I have had to forget."

"Georgina, I know you only care about me and want to spare me any pain, and I love you for it. But I promise I only want to glance through those things before you send them away. Who knows, there may be something there we would regret throwing out! And I feel no pain over Damien's doings now. I feel only pity for him."

Georgina still did not seem happy about it, but she nodded, and called out, "Bring that trunk back here for Lady Emily to see. She will send for you when she is ready for you to carry it away."

"Thank you, Georgie," Emily whispered. "This will not take me very long."

"I hope not. I am going to the nursery to look in on

Elizabeth Anne and Sebastian. Perhaps then we can go to the mantua-maker?"

"Of course." Emily watched Georgina turn away, then instructed the footman to place the old trunk near the windows. Only when the door closed behind the servants and she was alone again did Emily kneel beside it and raise the lid.

Tiny dust motes rose up, dancing in the sunlight, and she inhaled the old scents of the pine soap Damien used and stale tobacco and brandy. As she stared down at the jumble of clothes and papers, the garments she had rifled and pilfered only yesterday, she realized with a small shock that her words to Georgina were actually true. She felt no pain any longer when she thought of Damien and all the troubles he had caused. She had carried her anger around for years, like a small, hard stone in her heart. It weighed her down, causing such bitterness and confusion that she could not even fully appreciate all the fine things that were in her life.

But last night, in David's arms in the rich darkness, that stone just dropped away, and her heart could take wing again. Just as it had when she was a child and could dance barefoot in the country grass. The lonely years were behind her. Damien was dead, and she could only feel sorry for him. He had never, *could* never, have seen the truly valuable things in life as she did now. Jewels, money, position—they were as nothing. Love and family were all.

She loved David, and she wanted to give him a token of that passion, of all he meant to her. If her suspicions were correct, the perfect "token" might be right before her. It had always been here. She was just too blind to see it.

She had been blind to many things for a very long time. Now, there could only be light and truth.

Emily pulled the clothes out of the trunk, the papers

and old, string-tied bundles of love letters. She piled them up on her carpet, the detritus of a life ill-spent. As she leaned over to peer into the shadowed depths, she saw she had indeed been right—the interior of the trunk was far smaller than the exterior.

The dark blue velvet was old and worn, shredded in several spots. Emily dug her finger beneath one of the holes and pulled it away. Once the cloth was removed, she saw a thin, cheap wooden false bottom.

"Damien," she murmured. "You old cheat." Using a stout letter opener from her escritoire, she wedged up the board—and gave a satisfied sigh.

She *was* right. There, in a narrow compartment at the bottom of the trunk, was a treasure. A small treasure, to be sure, but far more than she would have imagined her reprobate brother could hold onto. A leather purse clinked with gold coins. A little box held loose, snow white pearls. In a velvet case, she found her mother's diamond tiara, a piece that had vanished from Fair Oak many years ago.

Emily smiled, imagining her mother's joy when it was presented back to her.

As she put the tiara aside, her gaze fell on another pouch, tucked in the darkest corner. Holding her breath, feeling her heart pound like thunder in her breast, she grasped the pouch and pulled it out of the trunk.

The Star of India spilled out onto her palm, casting a twilight blue glow over the white fabric of her skirt. *This* was the real Star—she knew it as well as she knew her own name. It was warm on her skin, the facets seeming to whisper and murmur as she turned it over on her palm. It vibrated with a magic all its own.

The Star was rougher cut than the paste copy and Mr. Jervis's excellent sapphire. The whiteness of the surrounding diamonds was muted, and the gold setting was dull. But she had never seen anything lovelier—except for David's dark eyes, and the sheen of his daughter's black hair.

She was not a superstitious person. But still, she had only one thought as she folded her fingers tightly over the true Star. *Safe*. They were all safe now.

The jewel would soon be back in the hands where it belonged, and it could never hurt anyone ever again. Emily slammed the lid of the trunk down, catching the past in its dark, dusty depths.

Chapter Fourteen

*D*avid stared up at the façade of the Kentons' grand townhouse before he reached for the polished brass door knocker. The building was quiet in the late morning light, seeming deserted except for the clatter of coal from the servants' entrance. It was full early for calls— but David had never proposed to a lady before, and found himself impatient to commence. He knew that he could expect a favorable answer from Emily herself. But what about her ducal brother? What would he say to the "Indian earl" paying court to his sister?

He raised the knocker and brought it down with a hollow, purposeful thud. The door handle clicked, and, much to his surprise, he was faced not with a stern butler but with Emily herself. Her smile glowed with a radiance he had never seen; summer sunshine itself poured forth from her pale curls and pink cheeks.

"David!" she gasped, clutching his hands in hers and pulling him into the foyer. As soon as the door shut behind them, she looped her arms about his neck and went up on tiptoe to kiss him. "I have missed you so much."

He laughed, tightening his clasp to hold her against him. "We only parted a few hours ago. You did not have time to miss me, *shona*." Of course, he had missed her, as well, though he would not say it aloud. It seemed absurd to miss someone seen only the night before. But there it was. Something had happened while they were locked in the close darkness of that closet. Something rare and profound. A destiny fulfilled at last.

If there *was* a curse on his family, as his grandmother believed, surely Emily's kiss had broken it. He felt free, and as young as the day when he first met Emily Kenton so very long ago.

"Nevertheless, it has been too long." She kissed his nose and his chin, giggling like a delighted schoolgirl. "I do think that you should—"

A discreet cough behind Emily interrupted her. She swung around, her arms still around David's neck.

"Oh. Hello, Alex dear," she said, her voice just the slightest bit more subdued.

David untangled her arms and turned toward her brother, holding her hands in his. The duke's face was utterly unreadable as he observed the scene his sister was creating in his own foyer. There was no frown, no smile—just the blank marble of a Roman statue.

"Good morning, Your Grace," David said, with a polite bow. "I hope it is not too early for a—business call."

"Certainly not," was the reply, made in coolly measured tones. "Depending what that business is. I have been expecting you, Lord Darlinghurst. Perhaps you would care to step into the library? If you will excuse us, Emily."

Emily nodded, her curls bobbing. As she stepped back, she whispered, "After you speak to Alex, David, meet me in the drawing room. I have something to give you."

David raised her fingers to his lips for a quick kiss. Something to give him, eh? That sounded promising, indeed.

Emily paced the length of the drawing room, sweeping her fingertips over the tops of the marble and gilt pier tables as she went. She did not see the garden out of the tall windows, or the paintings on the walls or the ornaments scattered on the tables. She just turned at the end of the room and paced back.

David was spending an inordinate amount of time in the library with Alex. Much longer than it should take. Was there a problem of some sort? What was happening in there? She wished she dared go eavesdrop at the door. She also wished Georgina was here to reassure her, but her sister-in-law was upstairs dressing to go to the mantua-maker. Even Elizabeth Anne and Sebastian were occupied with lessons and napping. Emily was quite on her own.

Or perhaps not entirely on her own. She opened the little pouch she held tucked in her hand and peered down at the Star's flash of blue fire.

Had it truly been only a few days ago that she was so overcome with a strange, restless melancholy she could not explain? When she listened to Georgina express worries about her failure to find a suitable match? That seemed so far away now—part of another life, another Emily. Her heart was still now, bathed in the same blue light of serene happiness and belonging she saw in the Star. It was David who made that happiness. David who showed her in so many ways—especially in the way he so gamely went along with her wild schemes—that they belonged together. Had always belonged together.

He made her laugh; he made her life seem merry again, when she thought she had lost the capacity for such untainted joy long ago. She saw the future now, not as a vista of the same meaningless balls, routs, and polite conversations and cruel witticisms, but as a series of endless possibilities. She and David and Anjali—and whoever might choose to come along later—would be a true family.

A tiny, nervous flutter ached deep in her belly, and Emily pressed her hand hard against it. All that would happen only if Alex gave David his blessing. But why would he not? He and Georgina had been wanting her to wed for the longest time!

Yet they *had* been in the library for an hour at least. Surely more than that—hours and hours! Were she and David going to be forced to make a dash for Gretna Green?

Curling her fingers tightly around the Star's pouch, Emily paused before one of the windows to stare out at the garden. Elizabeth Anne was there now, walking with her nursemaid, the sun turning her long red curls to molten fire. She waved up at her aunt, beaming.

Her niece's smile lifted Emily's spirits again. As she waved back, she heard the drawing room door open behind her, and she spun around to see David there. For an instant, his face seemed so solemn and serious that her heart sank once more. Then, he grinned—and the whole room, the whole world, flooded with light.

Emily dashed into his arms, and he lifted her off her feet, laughing.

"Well?" she demanded impatiently. After all, she had waited for this very moment since she was a little girl.

David just smiled. "Lady Emily Kenton, will you do me the great honor of becoming my wife?"

"Yes!" Emily cried, and kissed him. Once, twice, three times.

David chuckled through their kisses, the sound vibrating warmly through her. "Now, Em, I had an entire speech planned about how I intend to spend the rest of my life making you happy. I was going to go down on one knee and declare my undying devotion. Anjali has assured me, most solemnly, that ladies adore it when a gentleman goes down on one knee to propose."

"I do not need declarations of undying anything," Emily said stoutly. "You more than proved your devotion by hiding in that cupboard with me last night,

when any other man would have sent me directly to
Bedlam. All I need, David—all I have ever needed—
is you."

"Just as I need you." Their lips met again in a kiss of
such tenderness that it seemed eternal, made of all the
love that had come before them—David's parents, her
parents, Alex and Georgina—and all the love that would
go on long after they were gone. "I love you, my brave
Boudicca."

"And I love you. *Ami tomake bhalobashi.*"

"*Ami tomake bhalobashi.*"

Emily stepped back from his enticing kisses, taking
one of his hands between both of hers. "I have something for you, David. An early wedding gift of sorts."

"I thought the bridegroom was meant to give the bride
a present, not the other way around."

Emily shook her head. "You gave me back my necklace and earrings, my precious birthday gift. That is all
the present I need. And what I have to give you is not so
much a gift—it is not really mine to give. It is more of
a return. A putting to rights."

David's brow creased in puzzlement. "What do you
mean?"

Emily removed the Star of India from its pouch and
placed it carefully into his hand. "I believe this belongs
to you."

David stared down at the jewel, turning it over so that
its facets again flashed. It sparkled even more radiantly
than before, as if rejoicing in its freedom after such a
long confinement. As if it rejoiced at being home.

But David was silent for several long moments—so
silent Emily could almost vow she heard her own heart
pounding.

He raised his gaze to hers, the dark depths of his eyes
unreadable. "Where did you get this? How long have

you had it?" His voice was quiet, but thrummed with a
barely leashed power.

"Only since this morning," Emily hurried to explain.
"Georgina was tossing out some of Damien's old things,
and I realized that there was something not quite right
about one of his trunks. It was hidden in a false bottom.
He had never sold it at all." Her own gaze dropped to the
Star. It was so very lovely, resting there on David's hand.
But was there truly a malevolence hidden in its glorious
depths? "I vow to you, David, I did not know it was
there! I would never have gone to the lengths I did, had
I known. I just thought—"

Her words escaped her as she was suddenly caught in
a tight embrace, David's arms around her, holding her as
if he would never let her go.

"Em," he muttered roughly. "He never deserved such
a sister as you. *I* do not deserve such a wife as you. My
darling, clever Boudicca."

Emily laughed from sheer relief and utter joy. All was
right—she and David *would* marry, and the Star was in
its proper place. "So, we shall not be cursed, now that
the Star is back? The cows and chickens at Combe
Lodge won't wither away, and Anjali won't grow up to
hate us for being dreadful parents and elope with her
dancing master?"

David threw back his head and laughed. "No, Em. I
think any curse was lifted the moment I saw you standing there in that ballroom. We are together again. No ill
can come to us. My grandmother always quotes an old
proverb which says that a stick floats, as does a swimmer. It is the swimmer that the sea loves to bear, for he
has sensed its depths."

"Then I just have one question for you."

"And what might that be?"

Emily smiled at him. "*How soon* can we be married?"

Epilogue

India, Three Years Later

"Is it not beautiful, Mama?" Anjali whispered, leaning out of their open carriage as it made its slow progress down a narrow, curving road. Heavy, emerald green trees and thick vines twisted above their heads, casting flickering shadows over her black hair and white muslin dress.

In the valley below them, like an illusion or dream, was the great temple of Shiva, drifting on a fog-shrouded base of tangled blue-black vegetation and moss-encrusted ancient stones. Carved figures covered every inch of the façade, dancing and bathing ladies, warriors on horseback, elephants, and Shiva's bull, Nandi.

Emily put her arm around Anjali, leaning out beside her. "Oh, yes, my dear. It is beautiful indeed."

Beautiful was not adequate. It was—otherwordly. Since their arrival in India, Emily had seen many strange, exquisite sights—things she would never have thought she could observe outside of books. None of them could compare to this, but all were marvelous. Grand dwellings of white stone, their windows shielded from the hot afternoons by elaborately carved shutters; ladies fanning themselves on long terraces as they sipped *lassi* and watched servants building shrines in the overgrown gardens. Deer and gazelles bounding free along the lanes. Bright pink and orange and red flowers, which her maidservants twined in their hair.

She had tasted food unlike any in England: papaya which burst sweet and tart on her tongue, the spices of vegetables and tender meats, leavened by sauces of cooling yogurt. She had danced in moonlit gardens to music of such mystery and a deep, moving spirit.

She made love with her husband beneath a hazy mosquito netting, on mattresses spread with silk and strewn with flower petals. Afterwards, they would lie entwined in the night, the heavy, sweet-scented breeze cool on their heated skin, listening to the far-off music from the water. She thought then of the saying she had seen carved over an ivory screen at the Red Fort in Delhi—"If there is a paradise on earth, It is this, it is this, it is this."

It was an enchanted life—one she never could have imagined. One day, not very far off, they would have to leave it and return to the reality of their lives and responsibilities in England. But she would carry all of this in her heart forever. Along with the family who had brought her such splendors and made her life complete.

She hugged Anjali close to her. How tall her daughter was growing! Soon she would be a young lady in truth.

David's arm came about Emily's waist, holding her safe as the carriage jolted over the rough trail. The rains had not yet come to turn the path to impassable mud and muck, and it was baked to a stonelike hardness. His hand rested protectively over the slight swelling of her belly that was as yet the only outward manifestation of a blessed event still several months in the future.

Emily turned to smile at him, reaching up to cradle his cheek in her palm. He wore his Indian garb today, loose white cotton trousers and tunic, and his raven hair ruffled in the breeze. He grinned at her, looking as young and free as he had the first day they met, so many years ago, when his father brought him to tea with their new neighbors. But the gleam in his dark eyes spoke of a newer and very grown-up memory, of last night in their chamber.

"I have never seen anything like it, David," she murmured. "It is wondrous indeed."

"I am glad you approve, *shona*."

"How could I not? It is a fitting home for our treasure."

The carriage rolled to a halt several feet away from the temple's shadowed entrance, beyond a small pool that guarded the vast, forbidding portal. Anjali scrambled down the steps, pulling up the white straw bonnet that dangled down her back from its ribbons and tying it beneath her chin. As she stared up at the temple, wide-eyed in awe, her merry smile faded and her pretty face took on a solemn, almost prayerful aspect.

Emily felt that very solemnity deep in her own heart as she let David help her to the ground. This place held such mystery, an ineffable spirit that wrapped about her like incense smoke.

This was not the dwelling place of her own God, to be sure. But yet something *was* here, something that moved her, and she felt the presence of the sacred. She felt welcomed and blessed.

The closed carriage which bore David's grandmother, Meena, and her attendants came to a halt behind their own vehicle. Emily turned to watch the grand lady step down, swathed in a sari and veils of deep blue silk embroidered in gold. In her jeweled hands she held the small, elaborately etched silver box containing the Star of India.

It was truly home at last.

Meena nodded at David, and even to Emily. When

they first arrived in Calcutta, Emily had received the distinct sense that Meena did not care greatly for her new granddaughter-in-law. But, in recent days, she had thawed a bit—especially when she was given the news that Emily was expecting a happy event.

"*Lokhi mei,*" Meena called to Anjali. "Come, walk in with me. Take my arm."

Anjali hurried forward to slide her hand into her great-grandmother's crooked elbow, giving her support as they slipped off their shoes in front of the tall, carved doors.

"This is a momentous occasion," Meena murmured. "After this, my existence here is complete."

"But not until after you see the new baby, *Didu,*" Anjali answered urgently.

Meena gave her a gentle smile. "No. Not until then." She nodded at David, who stepped forward to knock at the doors.

Emily scarcely dared to breathe as the portals slowly, achingly slowly, swung open, as if pushed by unseen hands. She shivered in spite of the cashmere shawl draped over her shoulders. She had not felt such nervous tremblings since the day she walked down the long aisle at St. George's, Hanover Square, and took David's hand in hers, as she did now. She slipped her fingers into his warm clasp, and together they moved into the temple.

A more different space from St. George's could scarcely be imagined. The room was cavernous, as vast and cold as the stone it was carved from. The walls and ceilings were covered with even more carvings, more dancing figures and embracing couples, arching around them in a living, writhing mass. At the very end, in a high, gilded niche lit by hundreds of candles and with dozens of flowers tossed at its dancing feet and garlanded about its neck, was a statue of Shiva. The god of stillness and dance, bounty and wrath, destruction and

fertility—all the contradictions of life. He was gilded
and shimmering, with a diamond the size of a pigeon's
egg set in his forehead and pearls looped amongst all the
flowers.

In the flickering light, he almost seemed truly to
dance with joy that he had the Star back in his possession
at last.

Meena and Anjali walked up to the jade base of the
statue and bowed deeply. Meena chanted some low,
keening prayer, her voice echoing to the very ceiling and
beyond to the sky.

Emily took this all in, fascinated, but she shrank back
in the shadows. This was a part of her—the Star had
preoccupied her thoughts for so long, had even, in a way,
brought her together with David again. But her part in its
history was finished. She had found the Star for David,
so he could fulfill his vow to his grandmother. Now it
was done. The rest of her life could begin.

"You should go with them," she whispered to her husband.

"Will you be all right?" he asked.

"Oh, yes, darling." She gave him a reassuring smile,
and squeezed his arm before letting him go.

She watched as he joined his grandmother and daughter at the feet of the statue. Emily's hands tightened in a
prayerful clasp while Meena lifted the lid of the silver
case and drew forth the Star. Meena's chanting grew
louder, and she raised the jewel high. The glow of the
candles reflected the blue depths. What would happen
now? Emily thought, aching with suspense. Would the
walls crumble? The roof cave in?

Nothing of the sort, of course. This was not one of
Georgina's Minerva Press novels. Meena's chant died
away, the reverberations of it lingering in the chill air.
Then—silence. A silence deeper than any Emily had
ever known.

Meena placed the Star into David's hands, and it was he who returned it to the god's golden feet. There it sparkled in an answering dance.

Meena fell to her knees in prayer, but David and Anjali came back to Emily's side. David put his arms around her, holding her close.

"It is done now, my love," he told her.

"*Didu* says that now the curse is lifted. Your son will live a long, happy life and bring you much honor. And I will marry a rich prince." Her small nose wrinkled at this last pronouncement.

Emily laughed gently. "Oh, will you truly, my dear? A prince?"

Anjali shrugged carelessly. "So she says. But I know that is not true."

"How do you know that, *shona-moni*?" David asked her.

"Because I am going to become a famous artist, like Aunt Georgina, and travel the world creating great works of stunning beauty," Anjali declared matter-of-factly. "There will be no time for any silly princes." With that, she turned and made her way back down the long expanse of the great temple, disappearing into the afternoon sunlight.

"I wonder where she got such a notion," David whispered.

Emily tipped her head back to stare up at him innocently. "I am sure I have no idea. At least she has given up the idea of becoming a great circus performer."

"Indeed. We must be grateful for every blessing."

"Yes. We must." Emily lowered her forehead to his chest, feeling the strong, reassuring rhythm of his heart against her skin. Her life was full of blessings, in truth. David, Anjali, the baby. And more. "David, my dearest."

"Yes, Em?"

"Is it really over? Truly?"

She felt his finger slide beneath her chin, lifting her gaze back up to him. "My grandmother's curse—mayhap. Our love—never." And he kissed her, his lips tender and passionate, promising forever in this place of ancient destiny.

It was a promise Emily intended to see was kept.

If you liked *The Star of India,*
you'll love Amanda McCabe's
next enchanting historical romance,
on sale in spring 2005

Read on for a preview . . .

Italy, 1819

"*I*s she dead?"

"How can I see if she is dead, Maria, when she's all twisted up like that? *Santi Giovanni.* Here, take her arm and help me move her."

The voices came to Katerina faintly, as if they echoed down a long, empty corridor. She wanted to open her eyes, but they were sealed shut, and her head throbbed so intensely she couldn't bear to move it. Every time she tried, stars burst in her brain, white-hot. She managed to open her hand flat and felt the wet stickiness of sand. The same coarse sand clung to her lips and cheek.

Slowly, she touched the tip of her tongue to her teeth and tasted the unmistakable coppery tang of blood.

Blood!

Where was she? What had happened?

Her mind was a whirling, twisting blank. She struggled painfully to remember, but the harder she grasped, the further it all slipped away. She was almost certain she had been at a party of some sort. There were vague echoes of champagne, music, laughter—a handsome pair of dark eyes gazing down at her admiringly. How had she gone from *that* to lying on a strange shore, with blood in her mouth and her head about to explode?

If only she could *remember . . .*

Then strong hands reached for her, turning her onto her back.

Another sharp pain cracked through her head. Even those fragile wisps of memories retreated with the force of that agony. Katerina gasped, struggling not to slip back down into that sticky darkness.

"She's alive, Paolo!" a woman's voice cried. "See, she is breathing."

"So she is, barely. There's a lump at the back of her head, and this cut on her cheek is deep."

A rough fingertip prodded lightly at her cheek, and she pulled away from the sting.

"She must be a fine lady," the woman whispered. "Look at her jewels, and this silk gown."

"All of her jewels won't save her if we don't get her to the doctor now," the man muttered. "You wait with her, Maria, while I fetch Gianni and the others. We can't carry her to the village ourselves."

A quiet moment passed, filled only with the shrill of gulls soaring overhead, before Katerina felt a cool touch smooth the wet clumps of her hair back from her face. She smelled the distinctive odors of fish and lemon, as well as the salty tang of the sea. Somehow, those familiar, earthy scents were comforting, and calmed her.

"Can you hear me, *cara*?" the woman said.

Katerina spat out a mouthful of sand and blood. Painfully, she forced a whisper through her raw throat. "*Si*. I hear you, *signora*."

"*Va bene!* You're awake. You mustn't worry about a thing. We will take you to the doctor. Just lie here."

Using every ounce of her strength, Katerina pried open her gritty eyes and stared up at the woman. It was a gray, cold day, but even that faint light hurt. The woman, an elderly peasant with silver threaded through her black braids and a stained white apron over her faded dress, was surrounded by a halo of the dazzle.

Katerine closed her eyes against it. *"Grazie,"* she whispered hoarsely. "Thank you for your help."

"Poor little one! How you must have suffered. Do you remember what happened?"

"No." Nothing but that echo of music—and a tall man who held her close as they danced. *My Beatrice,* he whispered. *You are far more lovely than Dante's beloved could ever have hoped to be.*

"Nothing? Not even your name?"

She did remember that. It was emblazoned on her mind like a beacon. "Katerina."

"What a pretty name. Katerina. I am Maria." Katerina felt the woman shift around. "Ah, here is Paolo and the boys! You will soon be at the doctor."

Katerina heard the shuffle of booted footsteps in the sand, the rustle of rough wool cloth. "I see she is awake now, Maria!"

"For now. She can't remember much, though. We have to get her to the doctor quickly."

"Si, si. Here, boys, help me lift her onto the litter."

Hands reached for her again, lifting her high into the salty air as if she were a load of fish. Katerina screamed out against the fresh sword stabs of red agony. Just when she knew she could take no more, that she would die of the pain, the world went dark at the edges. The thick blackness spread, until there was nothing at all.

England, One Year Later

Blood. So much blood.

It stained his hands, his clothes, soaked into his very soul as he lifted his wife's delicate, broken body in his arms. Caroline's golden hair spilled down in a rippling, sunshine wave, just as it always did, but her violet-blue eyes were glazed, sightless as they stared up endlessly at the sky.

Pain wracked his own body, stabbing at his face, his side, with white-hot blades. It was as nothing to the pain in his heart. He crawled to his wife, reached out for her, even as he knew she would be forever beyond his touch. The splintered wood of his own wrecked phaeton was between them. He pushed the ruins aside with his cut and bleeding hands, and dragged his wife across his lap. She fell limply against him.

"Caroline," he sobbed. "Caroline. This is my fault. I am so sorry—don't leave me! Caro, come back to me. Come back to me . . ."

Yet even as he buried his face in the bright cloud of her hair, she faded from his grasp forever. He tried to hold onto her, but she was gone.

Gone . . .

*   *   *

Michael awoke with a sharp gasp. "Caroline!" he called. There was no answer from the shadows of his bedchamber. Nothing but his own voice echoing back to him mockingly.

It was that dream again. The same dream that always came back to haunt him over the last long five years, just when he thought it was gone forever.

But it wouldn't leave. Not until he could forget that warm springtime day when Caroline died. And that would be never.

Michael rolled to his back, staring up at the underside of the bedcurtains. He took a deep, cleansing breath, and slowly came back into the reality of this room, this present moment.

"I am no longer that reckless boy," he muttered. That careless life, that wild existence of gaming and drinking and dancing and coarse affairs was buried with Caroline. He was no longer "Hellfire Lindley"; he was Mr. Michael Lindley, younger brother of the Earl of Darcy, respectable country landowner. He looked after his Yorkshire estate, took care of his family and his tenants and employees.

As far as he could get from the ballrooms and the stews of London.

Some days, when he was busy riding over his property, meeting with bailiffs, reviewing ledgers, he imagined—no, he *knew*—that that life was left behind. But in the night, it was a very different story. The past and all his mistakes were waiting for him.

Michael threw off the last hazy shackles of dream-sleep and pushed himself out of bed. His nightshirt was damp with the sweat of his nightmare. He tore it off impatiently and tossed it to the floor. Naked, he strode across to the room's double windows. He opened the casements and let the chill night air flood over him, bringing healing with it.

The moon was nearly full, casting a pale, greenish glow over the gardens below. Far off in the distance, he saw the tall spire of the village's ancient Norman church. It glowed like an otherworldly scene from one of the horrid novels his mother loved so much, as if restless, eternal spirits swirled amongst its tilting and moss-covered stones and angels. Yet on his own property, the gardens and fields of Thorn Hill; all was silent.

Michael leaned his palms against the wooden window ledge, not feeling the tiny, sharp splinters that drove into his palms. He stared at the cross atop that distant spire, reaching up to the moonlit heavens.

Silent.

He closed his eyes, absorbing the night's peace into himself. Tomorrow was sure to be a busy day. It always was, during springtime in the country. He should be sleeping. But he knew that sleep was very far away, even as the night worked its slow, calming magic on his roiling thoughts.

Then he heard a noise, a soft thud, from the chamber next door to his. It was so soft, it would have been imperceptible to most. But Michael was always attuned to what happened in that room.

He spun away from the window and snatched up a dressing gown from the foot of the bed. He was striding from the chamber even as he shrugged the velvet over his nakedness.

The door to the other chamber was unlocked, and a solitary lamp burned steadily on a low, round table. It flickered in the darkness, casting back the menacing shadows, throwing a soft light over the child peacefully sleeping in the pink and white canopied bed.

Or rather the child who *should* be sleeping peacefully in the lacy little bed. She had rolled out of it, as she sometimes did despite the bolsters on either side of her, and she lay in a heap on the pink carpet. Still slumbering.

Michael smiled at the sight of her thumb popped into her rosebud mouth, and he knelt beside her to lift her gently into his arms. She murmured quietly, her head rolling against his chest, but she didn't wake. He laid her back against the ribbon-edged pillows and tucked the blankets around her.

Her tangled golden curls, full of a milky-sweet little-girl smell, tumbled over her brow. He smoothed that hair back, hair so much like her mother's, and lightly kissed her cheek. Just the sight of her brought back a portion of that ever so elusive peace.

When they had first come to live at Thorn Hill, Amelia was frightened to be placed in an upper-floor nursery, so far from the grown-ups. Over her nursemaid's protests that he was spoiling the child, he moved her into the empty chamber next to his own. And he had never regretted it. Now he could soothe her bad dreams—and put her back into bed when she was restless in her sleep and fell.

"Sleep well, Amelia dearest," he whispered. "Know that I will always be here to protect you."

As he could not protect her mother.